AUSTRALIA

NEW
ZEALAND

TASMANIA

TASMANIA

Devonport
Asbestos Ranges •
• Beaconsfield
• LAUNCESTON

• Franklin River
• Frenchman's Cap

• HOBART

NDIAN OCEAN

TASMAN SEA

Contents

Chapter 1	Remembering the Future	7
Chapter 2	Who's Got the Skull?	12
Chapter 3	Hot on the Trail of the Skull	18
Chapter 4	The Shadow	23
Chapter 5	The New, Improved Coxie	29
Chapter 6	The Wet-Suit Man	34
Chapter 7	Total Recharge	39
Chapter 8	Conversation with a Time-Traveller	46
Chapter 9	Empty Pockets	53
Chapter 10	A Warning	59
Chapter 11	A Police Officer Calls	66
Chapter 12	Interview with the Old Bat	73
Chapter 13	The Choice	81
Chapter 14	A Theft in Time	88
Chapter 15	Nerve-Burn	95
Chapter 16	Timedetectors	100
Chapter 17	Anomaly	106
Chapter 18	The Other Option	112
Chapter 19	Lucky Old James	118
Time Line		124
Magnified Time Line		125

Remembering the Future

It was just after New Year. I was sitting on my bed feeling weak and miserable when Mum came in. "Still tidying up your room, Tom?"

"Yes, Mum," I said. "Nothing else to do."

If I'd said that a couple of years ago, Mum would have told me to stop moaning and go for a bike ride or a swim. Today, she sat down beside me.

"You could go fishing," said Mum.

I thought about getting out my fishing things and digging for bait. I thought about baiting my hook. The way I felt, I'd probably drop the bait and stick the hook in my thumb. It all seemed to be too much trouble.

"I'll leave it, Mum," I said. "Maybe tomorrow."

Mum sighed. We both knew it wouldn't happen. If you'd told me a year ago that I'd turn down a fishing trip to tidy my room, I'd have laughed. A lot can change in a year.

Mum went out, and I started sorting through the box from under my bed. It was full of old jigsaw puzzles, odd socks, a stamp collection, a crash-helmet, and the roller-blades I got when I was eleven. I wouldn't be skating this summer, so I tossed the roller-blades on to the pile. Someone else might as well have them. I didn't want to be reminded of the things I couldn't do.

I tried to fit some of the jigsaw-puzzle pieces together, but my hands were unsteady. Angrily, I scooped the pieces on to the pile. Things were getting worse. Now I couldn't do a puzzle meant for a ninc-ycar-old.

I put my hands on my knees to stop them shaking. I was really scared.

I'd been feeling weak for months. I couldn't even remember exactly when it started, because it had come on gradually. First, I got pins and needles in my hands and feet. Then, I started getting clumsy.

"Your centre of gravity must be changing," Mum said. "You're heading for another growth spurt."

I didn't have a growth spurt, though. As a matter of fact, I didn't grow at all. I'd been feeling bad for about four months when I realized it wasn't going to go away. In fact, it was getting worse. Mum and Dad took me to see Dr Sands.

"I haven't grown," I said. "I can't even play football any more. I can't do anything."

The doctor examined me and said I was fine. "Cheer up, Tom," he said. "Make sure you get enough sleep and exercise, and soon you'll be right as rain."

I did as he said, but I got worse, so Dr Sands sent me to hospital for some tests. I won't tell you about that. It was boring and uncomfortable, and it didn't do any good at all.

I spent most of the year having tests and feeling worse and worse. The doctors agreed that I had some weakness in my muscles and nervous system, but they didn't know the cause or the cure. They also didn't seem to think it was serious.

"Try positive thinking, Tom," said Mum. "Imagine yourself feeling better and better."

I tried that, but I just got weaker. And now, in the early summer, I didn't feel like doing anything at all.

Right at the bottom of the things I was sorting, I found an old shoebox. Inside were some mangled bits of metal and a gun. It wasn't a normal gun, of course. It was a sol-shot. It looked like a plastic ray gun. It was a dull black, with buttons and a trigger. I thumbed the safety-button off and squeezed the trigger. Nothing happened. I hadn't expected anything to happen, so I put the sol-shot down on the desk by the window and stared at it for a long time. I was remembering the future.

That's impossible, for *most* people, but I could remember the future because I'd been there. That's where I got the sol-shot.

It happened like this.

When we were eleven, my friend Coxie and I went camping in the Asbestos Ranges. Using my dad's metal detector, we found some metal medallions and an opalized skull that was more than 5,000 years old. Scientists thought the skull was a hoax because it looked far too modern to have been buried in the ranges for all those years.

The medallions carried Coxie and me back in time and we met the skull's owner. Her name was Lizba Smith and she was the scientist who had invented the medallions. Lizba was from the thirty-second century – more than a thousand years into our future. In the future, there was great social and environmental upheaval. People were forced to give up all their luxuries – except their pets. Lizba's partner Palmer thought people should get rid of their pets, too. He wanted to use the medallions to travel back in time so he could kidnap or kill a politician named Kane, before Kane grew up to defeat Palmer's wishes. Palmer forced Lizba to take him into the past, but she took him too far into the past.

Palmer found Coxie and me with Lizba. He shot me with a sol-shot and kidnapped Coxie.

That might have been the end of us, but Palmer died soon after. I had to use Lizba's sol-shot to destroy her computer so no one else could use her research. Coxie and I got home safely, but Lizba died when she destroyed the medallions we'd used. All we had to remind us were the mangled medallions and Lizba's sol-shot. It didn't work any more, after I'd used it to wreck the computer, so I'd put it away and forgotten about it.

So far, that had been the biggest adventure of my life, travelling to the future with Lizba and Coxie, and helping to defeat Palmer's group. The way I felt now, I thought it might be my *only* adventure. I was wrong about that, though. While I sat there, remembering the future, a new adventure was already beginning, an adventure that would take me a long way in time, and closer to death than I like to remember.

Who's Got the Skull?

I closed my eyes and, of course, I went to sleep. I dreamt about Lizba's skull. Lizba had been from the future, but she'd died a long time in the past. Rain and erosion had scattered her bones, and all that was left were the medallions and her skull. You think of skulls as being funny or scary, but Lizba's skull wasn't like that. It was opalized and, when we found it, I thought Mum might like it for her display cabinet. The police took it, though, and we hadn't got it back.

I woke up feeling weak and miserable, and I had a headache. The sol-shot was still on my desk, so I stuck it in my pocket. It was dinner-time. I didn't feel hungry, but I went out to the kitchen.

"Tom, what would you say to a short camping trip?" said Dad.

I thought about camping. I thought about pitching tents, splashing in the creek, and climbing in the ranges. I wouldn't be able to have any fun. I'd just have to sit near the tent, pretending to enjoy myself. "No thanks, Dad," I said.

"Why not visit Coxie?" suggested Mum

I thought about Coxie. After the adventure with Lizba we'd drifted apart. Then, Coxie's mum had married Mr Watts, who used to teach us at school. That was a real surprise, because Mr Watts ran the Adventurers club, and you never saw anyone who hated adventures more than Coxie's mum. Perhaps she'd changed. Anyway, they'd moved to Devonport. Coxie had written to me a couple of times, but I hadn't written back, so I couldn't very well ask to stay with them now. Besides, Coxie's mum would make a huge fuss over me. "No thanks," I said.

I saw Mum bite her lip.

"There must be *something* you'd like to do," said Dad. "You can't spend the summer holidays sitting around feeling sorry for yourself."

I thought about it, but there didn't seem to be anything I wanted to do, except go to sleep. That was my worst day. It's pretty rough when you're only thirteen and you just want to go to bed and sleep.

"Tom?" prompted Mum.

"Oh, right," I said. "Dad, you remember that skull Coxie and I found?"

Dad looked astonished. "Who wouldn't remember being interviewed by the police? Not to mention the fuss the newspapers made. What about it, Tom?"

"Do you know who's got it now?"

Dad frowned. "I don't really know. It's probably on display in a museum by now."

"If it were in a museum, we'd have heard," I said. "They'd have to tell us. After all, we found it."

"That's true," said Dad.

"They could at least put a card in the case," I said. "Saying who found it."

"Possibly," said Dad. "But it might be in the science department at the university, or still with the police. Why the sudden interest, Tom?"

I shrugged. "You mentioned the Asbestos Ranges just now, and that's where we found the skull."

"We could go and see what else we can find," said Dad, hopefully.

"Come on, Dad," I said. "Everyone's been detecting there now. There's nothing left to find. Still, I'd really like to know what happened to that skull." I prodded at the food on my plate.

"Why don't you try to find out, Tom?" suggested Dad. "Make it your project for the holidays."

I started to shake my head. "I can't be…"

"No!" said Mum. "No, Tom Stratton! Don't you dare say you can't be bothered!" She jumped up and grabbed a pencil, a pad, and the cordless phone and plonked them down in front of me. "Get started," she said tightly. "Start phoning and find out who's got that skull.

Do it *now*. Insist on being told. It's your moral right to know, and it's *my* moral right to see my son showing a bit of life!"

Dad and I stared. Mum doesn't often blow her stack like that. "Better do as she says, Tom," Dad said, shaking his head. "Or it might very well be *your* skull that ends up in a museum."

"Sure," I said. "The boy who wouldn't grow."

Mum left the kitchen in a rush, and Dad started stacking the plates. After he'd gone, I sighed. I knew it would take more energy to resist Mum than it would to do as she said.

First I phoned the local police station. It took three tries, but in the end I got through to Sergeant Kerry, one of the police officers I'd met before. "This is Tom Stratton," I said, making my voice deep so he'd take me seriously.

"Yes?" Obviously, he hadn't a clue who I was.

"Tom Stratton," I repeated. "I was one of the people who found that opalized skull out in the Asbestos Ranges. It was nearly two years ago. Do you remember?"

"I remember now. What can I do for you, Tom?"

"I want to know who's got the skull," I said.

Sergeant Kerry said he didn't know.

"You must know," I said. "You took it. You must know what you did with it."

"We did take charge of it at the time," he said, "but as no crime had been committed, it isn't our responsibility any more."

"But where is it?"

15

"That's a bit difficult." He sounded slightly impatient. Probably, he'd rather be out solving crimes, but public relations meant he had to be polite to me.

"I need to know," I said, trying to sound firm and responsible.

"Try the university," he said doubtfully. "Or the Yarra Museum. I think they had it at one time."

I thanked him, and phoned the university. They said to try the Yarra Museum. That meant a toll call, and I imagined the dollars adding up on the phone bill as they passed me from department to department. Finally, I was connected with someone who told me they *had* had the skull. They'd been testing and investigating it, but a local anthropologist had said they couldn't keep it because it had been discovered in Tasmania. The anthropologist had threatened legal action if they didn't give it back.

"Do you know his name?" I asked.

"Oh, yes," said the museum assistant, sourly. "I know her name, Dr Sylvia Pennyfather."

"I suppose you can't give me her address?" I said.

"I shouldn't," he said, and he gave me her address.

Hot on the Trail
of the Skull

The address was in Devonport, Coxie's new town.
I couldn't find Dr Pennyfather's phone number in the
directory, and the operator told me it was unlisted. And,
no, I couldn't have it.

I decided I would write to Dr Pennyfather and offer
information about the skull in exchange for news on its
current whereabouts. I asked her to phone me.

I waited for more than a week. During that time, I
took a long look at myself and I didn't like what I saw.

I was feeling feeble and tired, but surely I could do
something. So I did do *something*. Really heroic stuff!

I took the dog for a walk. It was only two blocks and, when I got home, I felt as if I'd run a marathon, but it was better than sitting around.

I went for a walk every day that week. It didn't make me feel better, but it didn't make me feel worse, either. All that time I waited for a reply from Dr Pennyfather. I really wanted to know what had happened to Lizba's skull. You see, I admired Lizba, because Lizba hadn't given up. Even when she was dreadfully injured, Lizba had done what she had to do. If I gave up now, I'd be letting her down.

Eventually, I got fed up and decided to go and visit Dr Pennyfather.

"I'll drive you," said Mum, when I told her my plans.

"Thanks, Mum," I said, "but I'd rather take the bus."

"Are you sure you can manage, Tom?"

"Look, Mum, I'm thirteen," I said reasonably. "I've only got to get on and off the bus, then walk a couple of blocks."

"What if she isn't there?" said Mum. "You'll have a long wait for a bus to get back home."

"Then I'll go and see Coxie," I said.

Mum nodded reluctantly, then telephoned Coxie's mum, Mrs Watts, and arranged for me to visit Coxie while I waited for the bus. There was a lot of noise in the background, and I could hear Mrs Watts raising her voice so Mum could hear.

"What was all that?" I asked, when Mum had hung up. "It sounded like a chain-saw. Or was it that mad bird, Cracker?"

Cracker is Coxie's cockatoo, and he loves the sound of his own voice.

"That was Coxie's baby sister," said Mum.

I didn't know Coxie had a baby sister. I couldn't imagine Coxie's mum and Mr Watts with a baby. Especially not a baby that sounded like a chain-saw.

"Perhaps I won't go after all," I said.

"But you're hot on the trail of the skull! You can't give up now."

"Can't I!" I muttered, but I knew Mum was right. I was committed to finding Lizba's skull. I had another reason for this visit, too. Since anthropologists study the human race, they have to have open minds and be interested in new ideas. Dr Pennyfather just might know how to cure my muscles.

I put on clean clothes, because I wanted to be taken seriously. I also put the sol-shot in my pocket. I'd never shown it to anyone but Coxie, but I thought Dr Pennyfather might be interested in an artefact from the distant future. Not that I'd tell her it was from the future, exactly. Not unless she seemed ready for the idea. At the last minute, I scooped up the mangled remains of the time medallions. They were ruined, but they were made of an unknown alloy, and I thought they'd interest her, too. I was right in a way. She became interested. *Too* interested! But you can blame a nut named Baz for that.

Mum drove me to the bus-stop. "No sense in getting tired before you start," she said. She handed me her mobile phone. "Just in case you need to call Coxie's mum. I wish Dr Pennyfather knew you were coming."

"Well, the worst she can do is tell me to go away," I said. "And why should she? She's a student of the human race, right? I'm part of the human race!"

"Yes, you are, Tom," said Mum.

I got off the bus in Devonport, and looked around. It was the first time I'd been out on my own for months. (You can't count walking two blocks from your own home as going out.) Dr Pennyfather lived in a cul-de sac off one of the main streets. Her house was surrounded by high stone walls, and a sign warned me the property was protected by an alarm system.

There was a big wooden gate in the wall, with metal spikes on top and an electronic lock. I knocked, but there was no answer, so I turned to a square intercom set in the wall. There was a sign over it that read DELIVERIES. I was delivering myself and some information, so I pushed the button with my thumb, and after a minute there was a squawk next to my ear: "Hwizzet?"

"I've come about the skull," I said, as slowly and plainly as possible.

There was a loud buzzing sound and the gate's lock opened.

The Shadow

Dr Pennyfather came out to meet me. She was short, middle-aged, and very ordinary, with piled-up brown hair and a long nose. She looked at me as if I were a flea.

"You're not Dr Kane!" she said.

"I never said I was."

"You said you'd come about the skull." For a student of the human race, she didn't seem very friendly.

"Yes, I did. My name's Tom Stratton. I wrote to you ten days ago, asking about your plans for the skull."

"I remember," she said. "Why are you here?"

"I came because you didn't call me."

"Quite so," said Dr Pennyfather. "I didn't call you because I didn't want you to come."

"This won't take long," I said. "I really just want to know..."

"You want to know all about my work so you can write some school project," broke in Dr Pennyfather. She sighed, then continued, "I've heard it all before! I have informed the local school that I am not available for interviews. Now it appears I must inform your school as well. Some people are extremely inconsiderate."

"This is nothing to do with school," I said. "It's about the skull. The Yarra Museum said you had it."

"So?" She raised her eyebrows over squinty, little eyes.

"I'd just like to know what you're doing with it," I said. "I was the one who found it, you know." Actually, Coxie was the one who really saw it first, but I didn't want to confuse the issue.

"So?" she said again.

"I *found* it!" I said. "If it hadn't been for Coxie and me, you wouldn't have even seen it! I can give you information you can't get from anyone else."

She gave me a dirty look. "There is nothing you can tell me. Archaeology is not a game for amateurs. Untold harm is done every year by unqualified persons doing precisely what you have done. Digging up priceless remains! Handing them over to the police! I'm surprised you didn't play soccer with it!"

I lost my temper. "I know a lot about that skull that you don't know," I said. "I can tell you whose it was, and what she looked like. I can even tell you when she was born."

Dr Pennyfather looked at me coldly. "You are talking nonsense. Get off my property."

"At least let me see it," I said.

"Absolutely not! The specimen is safely packed away. Now leave, before I call the police."

My hands were shaking, so I tucked them into my pockets. I felt tired and dizzy. I hated the thought of Lizba's skull being poked at by this woman. It wasn't dignified and it wasn't right. "Why don't you use this mobile phone to make the call?" I offered. "Tell Sergeant Kerry what you just told me. Ask him if *he* played soccer with the skull." I held out the phone, but she pushed my hand away. "If you're not interested in knowing about the skull's origin, how about these things from the same period?" I pulled out the ruined time medallions from under my handkerchief.

"I am not interested in your pieces of rubbish," she said. "The only interest I have in *you* is in your absence."

"Right!" I said. "I'm going!" I felt like pulling Lizba's sol-shot out of the other pocket and waving it at her. It wouldn't have hurt her (or so I thought), but it would have given her an awful shock. But then she really might have called the police, so I decided to ignore the temptation. As it turned out, that was a good thing!

After Dr Pennyfather had locked the gate behind me, I stuck out my tongue. So much for her! I leaned against the wall until I felt a bit better, then I set off for Coxie's place, taking a short cut through the busy mall.

It wasn't very far, but I had to keep stopping to rest. I pretended I was window-shopping. That's how I found

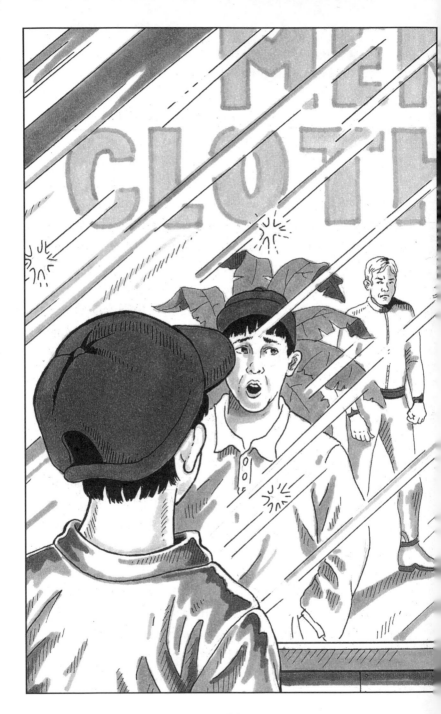

out that a man was following me. Every time I stopped, so did he, and I kept catching his reflection in the shop-windows. He was wearing a slimline wet suit, which wasn't as weird as it sounds. There are heaps of good beaches near Devonport. Still, it was an unusual thing to be wearing down town. I thought I'd seen him before, but I didn't know where. And if he *didn't* know me, why was he following me? Had Dr Pennyfather sent him to keep an eye on me? That would be crazy, but Dr Pennyfather did seem a bit odd.

I decided to shake him off, but it wasn't so easy. I tried ducking in and out of shops, but he stuck to me like glue. There wasn't much he could do to me in a crowded mall, but I was getting fed up, so I went into the next shop and approached the checkout.

"That man's following me," I said. "The one in the wet suit. See? He's just come in. I think I've seen him before somewhere, but I don't know him. Is there any way I can get out the back?"

"Are you pulling my leg?" asked the assistant.

"Of course not!"

"Our store detective's over there. He'll help you."

"He might not mean any harm," I said.

"Better safe than sorry," she said. "Are you all right? You look pale."

"I'm all right," I said. I wasn't, but there was really no use telling her that. The store detective headed off the wet-suit man, and I went out through the back way.

I'd lost my shadow, but the funny thing was, I felt more scared now than I had before. I even thought about using the mobile phone to call the police, but what could I say? A man in a wet suit had walked behind me, looking in the shop-windows? He'd followed me into a shop? So what? He hadn't threatened me.

I had awful stitch in my side, and my legs felt ready to drop off, but I kept on going. Five minutes later, puffing and panting like mad, I was knocking on Coxie's front door.

The New, Improved Coxie

I almost didn't recognize Coxie. He used to be little and skinny, but now he was a head taller than me, and much wider, too. His floppy hair was the same, but his chin was longer, his nose was bigger, and he had light down on his upper lip. And I'd never had to look up at Coxie before. "Coxie?" My voice squeaked with surprise.

"Hi, Tom." His voice sounded different, too.

I couldn't tell if he was pleased to see me or not. The old Coxie would have been grinning all over his face. This new, improved version was looking as if I wasn't quite what he'd expected.

"You're bigger," I said.

"You're not," said Coxie.

He said something else, but his voice was drowned by a chain-sawing noise from the next room. Coxie made a face. The chain-sawing noise was joined by shrieks and squawks and a noise like a wet sheet being shaken in the wind. I followed Coxie into the living room. The noise was even worse in there, but Coxie's mum didn't seem to mind. She was cuddling a bawling baby, and grinning at the cockatoo, Cracker, who was hanging upside down from his perch by the window, beating his wings and squawking. Coxie went across and stuck out his arm. Cracker shut up, flipped upright, and waddled up Coxie's arm to his shoulder. That cut the noise level by half.

"Tom's here!" yelled Coxie.

His mum smiled at me. "Hello, Tom." She patted the baby's back. There was more bawling, a burp, then silence, except for the ringing in my ears. Then Cracker said something I'd better not repeat.

"That bird," said Coxie's mum. "He starts every time Nattie does."

"How've you been?" asked Coxie.

"Not so good." I offered my finger to Cracker, but he hissed. He didn't remember me, and I wished I'd brought him an apple.

"What's wrong with you?" asked Coxie.

I shrugged. "I don't know exactly, but I don't think it's catching."

Coxie's mum gave him a warning glance. "It's good to see you, Tom. Any chance of you staying a few days? You and Coxie have some catching up to do."

This time Coxie gave *her* a warning glance. "Tom won't want to hang around the Noise Machine," he said, pointing to the baby. "Anyway, he's probably going camping with his dad."

"Not this year," I said.

"Your mum said you were seeing someone in town, Tom," said Coxie's mum.

"I came to see Dr Pennyfather, but she didn't like me."

"She doesn't like anyone," said Coxie. "She's just an old bat."

"Coxie!" said his mum. "Are you doing a project of some kind, Tom?"

"Not exactly. I'm trying to trace that skull we found. Remember, Coxie?"

After he'd been kidnapped by Palmer, Coxie had tried to forget our time-travel adventure. He'd tried to act as if it had never happened. I expected him to change the subject, but he nodded. "Sure. I've been thinking about that myself. Did you find out anything?"

"Not much," I said. "The police let it go to a museum, but Dr Pennyfather has it now. I went to see her but, unfortunately, she didn't want to see me."

Coxie's mum laughed. "That's her! Tell Tom what happened when you met her, Coxie."

Coxie shrugged. "I tried to interview her for social studies last year. She wouldn't talk to me though. If I'd known she had the skull I might have tried a bit harder. Did she show you the skull?"

"No way," I said gloomily. "She wouldn't even let me in the house."

"Let me show you the aviary," said Coxie, so we went out to the backyard. Cracker's new home was made of steel mesh. It had a lot of perches and swings, and food and water dispensers. It was a lot better than the rickety old cage at Coxie's old place.

"Gee, that's a parrot palace!" I said.

"It's thirty cubic metres," said Coxie proudly. "I'm going to get him a friend as soon as I can afford it."

"Who made the cage?"

"Wattsie and me, mostly," said Coxie.

"Great. What's it like, having your old teacher as your stepdad?"

"Wattsie's all right." Coxie grinned. "The Noise Machine's a pain in the eardrums, but if it was a toss-up between living with Wattsie and the Noise Machine or living with neither of them, I'd take both, anytime. Mum's so busy now she's given up fussing over me. Open that latch, will you?"

I had to use both hands, and it took ages to work it loose.

"Hurry up," said Coxie. "He's biting my ear. Ow! Cut that out, Cracker!"

"I'm trying," I said.

The door came open and Coxie tossed Cracker onto the nearest perch. The cockatoo gave a big whistle and climbed across to the food dispenser, where he started pushing sunflower seeds down his beak. Coxie shook his head. "Gee, you're in a pretty bad way, Tom," he said. "Are you always this weak?"

"No," I said. "Sometimes, I'm worse."

"Gee," said Coxie again. He really pitied me, and I felt like sinking straight into the ground. *I* used to feel sorry for Coxie, because of his asthma, and his dead dad and brother, and his fussing mum. Now Coxie was bigger and stronger. He had a new dad and a sister, and his mum had stopped fussing. Now Coxie was busy feeling sorry for *me.*

"How's your asthma?" I asked.

"Fine," said Coxie. "I grew out of it, I suppose."

"Lucky you." I turned away so he wouldn't see how envious I was.

"It's a funny thing you suddenly wanting to see the skull," said Coxie.

"What's funny about that, Coxie? You said you'd been thinking about the skull, too," I said. "Did you have any reason?"

"Yes," said Coxie. "I think someone's made some more time medallions."

The Wet-Suit Man

I stared at him. "How could that be? Lizba and I made sure that could never happen. The only medallions were the ones Lizba made, right? They melted when she died. And I destroyed her computer files."

"I know," said Coxie.

"So how *could* there be more? Palmer knew about them, but he died, too."

"Perhaps someone went back in time to before they were destroyed," said Coxie.

I laughed. "The only way to time-travel is to use the medallions. The only way to get the medallions would be to *use* the medallions, and the only way to use the medallions would be to *get* them. It's the chicken and the egg."

"A paradox," said Coxie.

"That's the word." I sat down in a garden chair. "So how could there be more medallions?"

"I can think of at least two possibilities," said Coxie.

"Well, go on, genius. Amaze me."

"If you're going to be like that, forget it!" Coxie glared at me, and I remembered that we'd disagreed about the medallions once before. That time I'd punched him. I'd been bigger than him, then. Now he was bigger than me. If he knocked me down now, I didn't think I'd be getting up.

"Sorry, Coxie," I said. "Tell me."

"It's like the difference between safety-pins and computers," he said.

"What?"

"Safety-pins were invented by one particular person," said Coxie. "We know who, and we know when."

"So?" I said.

"Computers don't have a single inventor," said Coxie. "Lots of people contributed to them. Most things are made by government-funded research teams these days, not by single inventors."

"That's right," I agreed.

"Sometimes," pursued Coxie, "two different teams invent the same thing independently. Boomerangs were used in different countries. The telephone was invented twice, and weren't there lots of Polar explorers at the same time?"

"So you think someone might have reinvented time medallions, not knowing Lizba had done it already."

"It could have been done at any time in the next twelve centuries," said Coxie. "Or it could have been done twenty centuries from now. If Lizba and Palmer could do it, why not someone else?"

I gulped. Time-travel sounds like fun. It sounds like a great chance to change history and fix up mistakes, but the adventure with Lizba and Palmer taught me what Coxie had known all along. Time-travel is very dangerous, for the people travelling, and for the people they meet. Time-travel can kill you.

"Point taken, Coxie," I said.

"It's also possible Lizba's files were copied before you wrecked the computer," said Coxie. "Palmer could have given them to someone."

"Palmer's dead," I said.

"Palmer," said Coxie, "hasn't been born yet. And what about all his friends?"

I groaned. "So, it *could* have been done. What makes you think it *has* been?"

"Well, I think I've seen someone from Lizba's time hanging around in the mall."

That really shook me. Time-travellers in the Asbestos Ranges is one thing. Time-travellers wandering around the mall is far too close to home. "Oh."

Coxie nodded. "I was down at the mall the other day and I saw this man in the arcade."

"Was he wearing a wet suit?" I asked.

"That's right. How'd you know?"

"I saw him, too," I said. "In fact, he was following me, today."

"Great, just great," said Coxie, glumly. "I suppose he's followed you here." He shot a look at the garden gate, as if he expected to see the wet-suit man loitering near the letter-box.

"No, he didn't." I told Coxie how I'd got the store detective to intercept the man. "He might be harmless, though," I said, "even if he is a time-traveller. After all, Lizba didn't mean any harm."

"Lizba did *her* time-travelling in the Asbestos Ranges, not the mall," pointed out Coxie.

"Maybe this man's a time-tourist."

"Who just happens to show up here and now? Who just happens to follow you through the mall? Come off it, Tom! That's too coincidental."

"What could he want?"

"I don't know," said Coxie, "but if he's anything like Palmer, he's after more than postcards from the past."

"I suppose so," I said gloomily.

Coxie stuck out his jaw. "We can't just sit around while this wet-suit man assassinates the prime minister, or Lizba's ancestors, or..."

"Or what?" I prompted.

Coxie looked embarrassed, and for a few seconds it was like having the old Coxie back. The old Coxie who was afraid of danger.

"Or what?" I repeated.

"Or us," said Coxie. "All right? I don't want to sit around while this wet-suit man decides to assassinate you and me."

I stared at him. "Why should he?"

"Because we know things we shouldn't know," said Coxie. "We know about time-travel, and we know about Palmer and what he tried to do to Kane. If we wanted to be really smart, we could put a stop to all that. We could leave a time-delayed message for Lizba so she never teams up with Palmer in the first place. Because of what we know, we could change the future."

"I would if I could," I said, "but there's no way kids like us can get hold of the technology we'd need."

Coxie sighed. "Right, Tom. But kids like us grow up. And who knows what technology might be available in twenty years? Things are developing all the time."

I looked down at my hands, which were shaking again. "Coxie, I don't think I'm going to live twenty years," I said. "I don't think I'm going to live *two* years."

It was the first time I'd admitted that to anyone, including myself. If I'd known how little time I really did have left, I'd have felt like dying on the spot.

Total Recharge

Coxie looked uncomfortable. "I thought you said the doctors didn't know what was wrong with you?"

"They don't, but it's getting worse," I said. "I haven't grown in more than a year, and I feel weak all the time. The doctors don't seem worried, but they don't know how I feel."

Coxie cleared his throat. "I'd better just try to sort out this wet-suit man by myself."

"What are you going to do?"

"I'll try to find out what he wants," said Coxie. "Without being obvious."

"I've still got Lizba's sol-shot," I said, "if that's of any use to you."

Coxie stared. "Gee! Why didn't you say so?"

"You didn't want to know before. And don't go getting any bright ideas about being a big hero. It doesn't work any more. The battery pack must be exhausted."

"I don't suppose you've got it with you?" asked Coxie, hopefully.

"Yes, I wanted to show it to Dr Pennyfather." I pulled the sol-shot out and flipped it to Coxie. But my hand was shaking again, so my throw was a bit off.

The sol-shot bounced on the grass and fired.

There was no bang and no flash. The sol-shots of the future don't make a bang or a flash. What they *do* make is a nasty mess of whatever they happen to hit. When Palmer shot me with one in the thirtieth century BC, I was paralyzed from the neck down for awhile. It was horrible, and thawing out was even worse. I don't think I've ever hurt so much! On another setting, sol-shots can be used to melt metal and plastic, or to scramble electronic circuitry. I hadn't bothered about the setting, because I thought it was dead. Only it wasn't.

The ray hit the edge of the aviary and the mesh glowed. Two links glowed red, then went black, then melted away.

Coxie let out a squawk of dismay. "What'd you do that for? You might have killed Cracker!"

My heart was beating wildly. "But it's been dead for more than a year!" I said. "It hasn't worked since it melted the medallions and the computer! Honestly, Coxie, I tried it a few days ago and I swear it was as dead as a dinosaur!"

"It isn't dead now!" snapped Coxie.

I shivered. I'd been carrying the sol-shot in my pocket with the safety-button off. I'd thought about waving it at Dr Pennyfather to give her a scare. If I had done that, I could have killed her, or myself. Just now I could have killed Coxie. And if I had killed Cracker, Coxie never would have forgiven me. I don't know what it is about sulphur-crested cockatoos, but the people who have them say they make the best friends in the world.

Coxie glared, then bent to look at the mesh. Cracker climbed down to look, too, then stuck his beak through the hole. "Get back in there, you nosy bird!" said Coxie, shoving him back. "Get some wire and the pliers from the shed, Tom. Quickly! I don't want him hurting himself on this jagged edge."

I fetched the wire and watched while Coxie quickly wove it in to replace the melted mesh. He didn't look at me again until he'd finished. "Dead as a dinosaur, right?" he said bitterly.

"It was!" I said.

"Then it's had a total recharge," said Coxie. "What'd you do? Plug it into an adaptor? Or did you stick in a a couple of batteries?"

"I didn't do anything!" I said. "I found it in a box under my bed, and it's been sitting on my desk for the past week. Just sitting there."

"In the sun?"

"Some of the time."

"It's solar powered," said Coxie. "I'll bet you." He seemed to have calmed down.

"You know I wouldn't risk hurting Cracker," I said "Or you."

Coxie grunted. "Let's put the safety-button on."

Very carefully, I picked up the sol-shot and pressed the safety-button. I checked by trying to fire it again, but it was safe now. "I'll drain it later," I told Coxie. "I'll put it back under my bed."

"Better to get rid of it," said Coxie.

"How? If I throw it away, some kid might find it. Who knows what would happen if I tried to burn it."

Coxie grinned suddenly. "A bit like a nappy or nuclear waste," he said.

"*What?*"

"You can't get rid of nuclear waste, and Mum says disposable nappies are practically as bad. You just can't get rid of them." Coxie paused, then added, "Well, come on."

"Where to?"

"The mall," said Coxie. "Let's see if we can find the wet-suit man."

"All right," I said. "But I warn you, I've about used up my exercise ration for today. You take the sol-shot, Coxie. My hands aren't too good. I'll leave the mobile phone with your mum."

Coxie tucked the sol-shot into his pocket, then stuck his head in the doorway and yelled out to tell his mum that we were going to the mall. In the bad old days, she would have warned him to put on a jacket, wipe his feet, and not to talk to strangers. Now, she just said she'd see him later.

43

"What time's your bus, Tom?" asked Coxie.

"About four," I said.

"Plenty of time, then. Got any money?"

I did, so we went down to the mall and bought some sandwiches and fruit juice, then sat down on the edge of the fountain to watch out for time-travellers. "What do we do if we *do* see him?" I asked.

"We'd better play dumb," said Coxie. "Convince him that we've practically forgotten all about it. That way he should give up any idea of getting rid of us... I hope."

"Sounds good to me. I wonder if he'll show up?"

"I suppose he..." Coxie didn't finish. Instead, he sputtered orange juice all over his front.

"Can't I take you anywhere without a bib, Coxie?" I said.

Still sputtering, Coxie jerked his head sideways. There, standing next to the fountain, was the wet-suit man.

He didn't look very threatening. I'd been nervous when he'd followed me earlier, but now that I was with Coxie, it didn't seem so bad.

So, what's the difference between people from the future and ourselves? Not a lot, because twelve or fifteen centuries isn't very long in evolutionary terms. There is something, though. Something. Maybe Dr Pennyfather could have explained it, if she'd been willing.

I looked at the wet-suit man for a couple of seconds, then I glanced at Coxie. He was busy cleaning up his shirt. When I looked back, the wet-suit man was gone.

Conversation with a Time-Traveller

"Hey!" I said. "Where did he..." I stopped, because suddenly he flickered back into view. He stepped around the fountain and came towards us, smiling as if we were old friends. "Hello, Tom!" he said. "Mind if I join you?"

"It's a free country," I said coolly. "How's the surf?"

"Unpredictable," he said. "I might win a few medallions though, if I'm lucky. You two wouldn't know anything about medallions, would you?"

"Not a thing," said Coxie blandly.

"I don't know you, do I?" I asked. He still looked a bit familiar.

"No. You *are* Tom Stratton aren't you?" The wet-suit man looked from me to Coxie and back.

"I'm Tom. This is Coxie."

"Hi, Coxie." He stuck out his hand, but Coxie didn't take it.

"Who are you?" asked Coxie. "What do you want?"

"Just to talk, Coxie." The man held up his hands. "See? I'm not armed."

I relaxed a bit more. We were armed or, at least, Coxie was.

"Why should you be armed?" asked Coxie. "Afraid of sharks in the mall?"

"Just joking." The wet-suit man grinned. "Pretty neat trick, Tom, alerting the store detective. It took me some time to talk my way out of that one. By the way, my name's Baz. Tell me, have you ever met Lizba Smith?"

Both Coxie and I jumped when Baz mentioned Lizba's name, but we kept our faces straight. "Who?" I said.

Baz smiled. "Oh, you'd remember Lizba, if you met her."

"Oh, yes!" said Coxie. "I remember Lizba. We met her ages ago, when we were little kids."

"Did she mention me?"

"I can't really remember," said Coxie bluntly. "I don't think so."

"Tom? Did Lizba say much to you?"

"Not that I remember." I tried to sound casual. "Like Coxie says, it was ages ago."

Baz shrugged. "Well, perhaps she had other things on her mind."

She had. Like preventing a crime. Like living long enough to do what was necessary. Like protecting the past and the future from time-travellers. Only it seemed as though she'd failed in that.

"How do you know Lizba?" I asked.

Baz laughed. "She's my mother."

That must be why he looked familiar, I thought. I was seeing a family resemblance. "What about Lizba?" I asked.

"She disappeared years ago," said Baz. "I'm anxious to find out what happened. Did she tell you her plans?"

I started to tell him she was dead, but Coxie hit me with his elbow. "She didn't say much," he said vaguely. "I've forgotten."

Baz smiled again. He seemed friendly, but Coxie obviously didn't like him much. "If you've forgotten, you can't help me," he said. "Pity. I'm trying to find out what happened to Lizba, and to further her work. I thought we could have helped one another. My mistake."

He got up and shrugged. "So, you can't help me and you don't want my help, right?"

"Right," said Coxie. "Sorry."

Baz smiled ruefully and stuck out his hand. "No hard feelings?"

It seemed to me that Baz was the one who might have hard feelings. If I'd been trying to solve a mystery about *my* mother I'd have wanted help. I felt bad about not telling him what we knew, but Coxie was right. We had to protect ourselves.

"I suppose not," said Coxie. He shook hands, then gathered up our sandwich wrappers and drink cartons and went to throw them in the rubbish bin.

I offered my hand. I tried not to let it tremble, but Baz noticed anyway. His smile faded. "Are you sure you don't want my help, Tom Stratton?" he said softly.

"What do you mean?"

"Well, that's a very bad case of nerve-burn you've got there."

"*What?*"

"Isn't that what's wrong with you, Tom?" asked Baz. "You seem to have all the classic symptoms of nerve-burn. Pretty far advanced case, too. I don't want to alarm you, but I don't think I've ever seen anyone so badly affected."

My legs gave way and I sat down again.

"Come on, Tom!" yelled Coxie. "We've got to go!"

"Wait a second, Coxie!" I called back. My heart was thumping with excitement or, possibly, with dread. "Right," I said to Baz. "What's nerve-burn? Can you cure it?"

"Trembling and progressive weakness," said Baz. "How old are you, Tom? Ten? Eleven?"

"Thirteen," I snapped.

"Then it's retarding your development and it's worse than I thought. What treatment are you taking?"

"None," I said. "The doctors don't seem to know what's wrong."

"A roboscanner would pick it up immediately!"

"What's a roboscanner?"

Baz made a face. "Oh dear, I was forgetting. Never mind, Tom. This is the twentieth century. You can't possibly have nerve-burn in the twentieth century."

"Why not?"

"It's caused by exposure to a type of ray gun that won't be invented for many years to come. I'm sorry if I've upset you needlessly." He patted my shoulder and walked away.

"Wait!" I said.

Baz glanced back.

"Wait, Baz!"

People stared, and Coxie came over in a hurry. "Cut it out, Tom. Let him go!"

"I've got to talk to him."

"We agreed…" began Coxie.

"Look," I said. "It isn't you who has nerve-burn. It's serious, Coxie!"

While we were arguing, Baz interrupted. "Well?" he said.

"Does that ray gun look like…?" I was about to pull the sol-shot out of my pocket, but I realized I'd given it to Coxie. "Coxie?" I said. He shook his head, so I described the sol-shot instead. "Is it black, and about this big, with a safety-button and a lumpy barrel?"

"That certainly sounds like it. But where could you have seen one?"

"I was shot by one of those when we were in the ranges," I said. "More than a year ago. Could that have caused nerve-burn?"

"I'd say it's a certainty," said Baz.

"You mentioned a roboscanner," I prompted.

"I shouldn't have," said Baz. "Like the ray gun that caused the problem in the first place, roboscanners won't be invented for centuries."

"Then I'm stuck with this disease?"

"I'm afraid so," said Baz. "Of course, there's just a chance I could… But, no, it isn't possible. If you boys could have helped me find Lizba, I might have been able to help you but, as it is, there's nothing I can do."

"That's blackmail!" said Coxie furiously.

"Nonsense!" said Baz. "I'd help Tom if I could, but without the medallions I can't."

I glanced at Coxie. "We've got to help him," I said. I turned to Baz. "All right," I said. "What is it you want to know?"

Empty Pockets

"It's simple," said Baz, "I need to trace Lizba, and I need her time medallions."

"I'm sorry," I said. "But Lizba is dead. She was afraid people would use the technology for the wrong purposes. She destroyed the medallions and herself." I explained to Baz what Lizba had done.

"So she nobly sacrificed herself to save the world," said Baz. "That sounds like Lizba! But you are quite sure she died?"

I nodded. "Yes, we found her skull in the Asbestos Ranges."

"How did you know it was hers?" asked Baz.

"She told us," I said.

"Where is this skull?"

"An old bat called Dr Pennyfather is studying it. She lives just a little way past the mall."

"I must see it," said Baz. "I must be certain beyond doubt that it is Lizba's."

"You'll never get it," I said. "Dr Pennyfather won't show you. Not unless you're another scientist. She wouldn't show *me*, and Coxie and I discovered it! She wouldn't listen, either."

Baz frowned, and I didn't blame him. I'd hate to think of someone studying my mum's skull. "I must get that skull," he said. "It would be worth... I mean, it would have great sentimental value to me. But I need the medallions if I'm to help you, Tom."

"You must have medallions yourself!" interrupted Coxie. "Otherwise, you couldn't have come here."

"I have a TDD – a time-displacement device. TDDs can be used by only one person." Baz showed us a thing like a wristwatch.

"You can't travel alone," said Coxie. "It kills you."

Coxie was certainly right about that. Lizba had died by travelling alone.

"Lizba's medallions were crude," said Baz. "The idea of being forced to travel in pairs is irresponsible. Using her system, a traveller ran the risk of losing a partner. Then, he'd be stranded, or forced to kidnap someone else!"

Coxie made a face. Palmer had kidnapped him for just that reason.

"How does this work?" I asked.

Baz hesitated. "When I redeveloped Lizba's original ideas, I made some modifications," he said. "I applied the same basic principle, but improved on it. I can travel alone, and since a TDD unit straps onto your wrist, there's no risk of losing a medallion and being stranded."

"So, why do you want the medallions?" asked Coxie. "You've superseded them."

"Yes, but Lizba's prototypical TDDs would prove very interesting to temporal scientists such as myself. They would make a valuable addition to our heritage," said Baz. "I also want to help Tom! My TDD will translate only one person through time, so to take Tom to a time when his condition can be cured, I need the medallions."

"You could go home and make another gadget for Tom," pointed out Coxie.

"Yes," said Baz, "but it would take me a great deal of time. And time is something Tom can ill afford. His condition could become critical at any…"

"I've got the medallions," I interrupted. "They're ruined, though." My insides felt as if I'd swallowed a lump of cold clay.

"Nevertheless," said Baz softly. "I'd like them back. Perhaps I could restore them."

"No," said Coxie loudly. "Lizba wanted the whole thing forgotten. We should respect that. Anyway, they're ruined, you can't use them to help Tom."

I had an idea. "Why don't you use your TDD to go to the time when the original medallions were in good working order?"

Baz looked surprised and nervous. I wondered why. Surely that possibility was obvious!

"You could go back to when Coxie and I had them both," I added. Then I had an even better idea. "After I'm better, we could help Lizba deal with Palmer. Then she won't have to die!"

There was a brief silence. Then Coxie turned to Baz. "Yeah, why don't you? I would if it were my mum."

Baz looked exasperated. "It isn't so easy," he said. "For a start, I'd be doubling back in my own lifetime. If I met myself, or if someone who knew me then met my current self, it could cause a paradox. No, the only chance is if I could meet Lizba in a time outside our natural lifetimes. Unfortunately, I don't know where, or when, she went. I could be searching the centuries for the rest of my life!" He spread his hands. "Even if the medallions are ruined, I might be able to use them to focus on a particular time and place."

"We could go to the Asbestos Ranges when I'm well again," I said. "We could go back and save Lizba."

"How could we?" said Coxie roughly. "You and I were already there, Tom. We didn't see our current selves, and we didn't see Baz. It's impossible."

"We could have been hiding," I said, but I saw that Baz and Coxie were right. Undoing what had happened to Lizba would be very difficult.

"The medallions?" repeated Baz. "I must have them if I'm to help you."

"They're in my pocket," I said. "Stop it, Coxie!" Coxie was tugging my elbow.

"Your friend doesn't trust me," said Baz.

"Listen…" said Coxie.

"No, *you* listen, Coxie!" I said. "You didn't want to use them, remember? They're mine now, and I'm going to give them to Baz." I reached into my pocket.

First, I pulled out a feather.

"That must be Cracker's," said Coxie.

Then I pulled out a handkerchief covered with a wad of chewing-gum. I felt in the other pocket, and pulled out fifty cents and a pencil. That was that. I'd run out of pockets. The time medallions were gone.

I felt really sick, the way you do when you sit down to do a test and you suddenly realize you're being tested on chapter five and you've only studied chapter four.

"The medallions?" said Baz again.

"I had them," I muttered. "They were in my pocket." I turned to Coxie. "You didn't take them, did you?"

"Of course not," said Coxie.

"They can't have fallen out," I said.

"You must have left them somewhere," said Coxie. "Did you leave them at my place?"

"No, I haven't had them out... Wait a minute! I was trying to show them to Dr Pennyfather, but she wasn't interested. I thought I put them back in my pocket, but maybe I dropped them instead. I was in a hurry." My hands had been shaking a lot, too, but I wasn't going to say that.

"So the medallions are in the same place as the skull?" said Baz.

"Probably." I groaned. I couldn't think of a worse place for them, except possibly the middle of the sea.

"Let's go," said Baz.

A Warning

"We'll show you where Dr Pennyfather lives," I offered, "but you'll have to do the talking. And get some different clothes first."

Baz touched the gadget on his wrist, and flickered out of sight. When we saw him again, he was wearing shorts and a bright shirt with the tag still hanging from the neck. "Better?"

Coxie and I stared. "You stole those from the shop, didn't you?" said Coxie.

"They're not real clothes," said Baz. "It's just a holographic illusion built into the suit."

They looked real to me. "What about the tag?" I said, pointing.

"Is that wrong?" There was another flicker and the tag was gone.

"I wish I could do that," I said. "Just think, Coxie. You could wear old clothes to school and look as if you were in uniform."

"What's the use of wearing old clothes if nobody can see them?" scoffed Coxie.

He had a point. I was still trying to come up with an answer when we reached the cul-de-sac where Dr Pennyfather lived.

By now it was late afternoon, and the wall looked really forbidding. It looked like the sort of wall a dragon might live behind – well, Dr Pennyfather *was* a bit of a dragon. "You'll have to use that squawk-box," I told Baz. "She doesn't like me and she would probably recognize my voice."

Baz pressed the button on the intercom. "Dr Pennyfather? I need to see you urgently."

After a short while, the gate opened, and Dr Pennyfather peered through. Coxie and I crouched behind the open gate. "What do you want?" she asked Baz, suspiciously.

Baz smiled. "Good day, I'm Dr Smith. We need to discuss some important artefacts that may have come into your possession."

"Any artefacts in my possession have been come by legitimately, and I have no obligation to discuss them with anyone."

"Not these. They were left here inadvertently."

"That is not my problem."

Baz stuck his foot in the gate as she tried to close it. "Perhaps I should get to the point, Dr Pennyfather. I believe Tom Stratton visited you today?"

"If you want to intervene for that tiresome little brat you're simply wasting your breath, Dr Smith," said Dr Pennyfather. "Amateurs! Let them make one lucky discovery and they think they can get away with murder!"

"How true," said Baz. "I am not here to speak on his behalf, but on my own. This morning, Tom Stratton had some valuable antique medallions that belonged to my mother. I think he hoped they would impress you. Did he show them to you?"

"No," said Dr Pennyfather.

"Then he must have disposed of them on your premises, for they were not in his possession when I apprehended him this afternoon."

"You'd better leave," said Dr Pennyfather. "This has nothing to do with me."

"May I be allowed to make a quick search? I cannot believe a scientist such as yourself would allow unique anthropological artefacts to fall into the wrong hands."

Baz seemed to be blackening my character right and left! Then I peered around the gate and saw Dr Pennyfather's eyes narrow. She had squinty, little eyes at the best of times, and now they practically disappeared. "Unique anthropological artefacts?" she said.

"Exceedingly," said Baz. "Twelve centuries old, at least. It is imperative that I find them."

"Come on, then," said Dr Pennyfather. "But I warn you! I have surveillance cameras in the grounds."

"Excellent! We could study the film of Tom Stratton's visit and find out precisely what he did with the medallions." Still talking, Baz went through the gate.

"Now what?" asked Coxie.

"We'll have to wait," I said.

We waited for ages. I began to feel cold and scared. I hate depending on other people, and since I'd been ill I'd had to depend on a lot of people: Mum and Dad, my friends, the teachers at school, doctors, and so on. At first, I had depended on the doctors to make me well, but how could they help? How could they diagnose a disease that wouldn't exist for centuries?

Suddenly, I felt a bitter rush of disappointment in Lizba. She'd seen Palmer shoot me with the sol-shot. Why hadn't she warned me? I tried to think back. "Hey Coxie," I said. "Lizba didn't say anything at all about nerve-burn, did she?"

"Not that I remember," said Coxie. "I wasn't with you all the time, though."

"She didn't," I said. "I know she didn't. Coxie, why didn't she warn me about what was going to happen?"

"Maybe she didn't want to scare you," said Coxie. "Maybe you were just unlucky. Perhaps people who get shot have one chance in a hundred of getting nerve-burn."

"Oh, yeah!" I said. "More likely she didn't care what happened as long as I finished the job."

"There wasn't anything she could have done," said Coxie, but he didn't sound sure.

"Anyway," I said. "Why did she make me destroy the computer if she'd already given her notes to Baz?"

"Weird," agreed Coxie. "She died so that no one would have the medallion technology, but she'd already handed it over. *If* Baz is telling the truth."

"Perhaps she didn't count Baz," I said. "After all, he *is* her son."

"So he says," said Coxie. He looked at his watch. "It's nearly four!"

That put me in a spot. Even if I hurried I'd probably miss the bus, and there was no way I wanted to leave now. "Do you think your mum would mind if I stayed the night?" I asked.

Coxie gulped. "Well…"

"You don't have to sound so pleased," I said rather sarcastically. "You've stayed with me plenty of times."

"I'm going to the movies tonight," said Coxie.

"I can still stay at your place," I said. "I don't feel like going out, anyway."

"I suppose we can ask," said Coxie. "Let's go."

"What about Baz?"

"Leave him a note," suggested Coxie.

I dug out a pencil and Coxie handed me a crumpled piece of paper from his pocket. I smoothed it out, and wrote a note to Baz. I added Coxie's phone number and asked Baz to call as soon as he could. I stuck the note to the intercom with chewing-gum.

"He won't know how to use a phone," said Coxie.

"He can use TDDs, so a phone won't give him much trouble," I said.

But Baz didn't phone. He was waiting for us right outside Coxie's garden gate.

"How did you get here so soon?" asked Coxie.

Baz flickered like a faulty light-bulb. "No time to talk," he said. He flickered again. "I've got the medallions, and I have to go..." He waved the medallions in front of me.

"What about my nerve-burn?" I yelled.

"I haven't forgotten, Tom. Listen, you might meet two other travellers. Don't believe anything they say about me. They're my enemies."

"What?"

"They're Palmer's friends." Baz flickered again, and this time he disappeared.

A Police Officer Calls

"Palmer's friends!" I groaned, loudly. "I don't like the sound of that."

"Perhaps we should stay home tonight," Coxie said.

"That's no good," I said hollowly. "They can catch us anywhere."

"Wonder where Baz just went?" said Coxie.

"Wonder *when* he went, you mean," I muttered. You can't use time-travel to move in space, you can only move in time. You can still disappear and appear in different places, though, by going forward or backwards in time, moving to a new place, then returning to the present.

"That gadget of his is more accurate than the ones we had," said Coxie. "He turned up just as we got here."

"I hope Palmer's friends don't come here," I said, "I suppose they're after Baz because he's Lizba's son."

"I wish Baz didn't know where I live," grumbled Coxie, "and what if Mum saw him disappear?"

"She'll think her eyes are playing tricks." I wanted to get inside before I collapsed.

Coxie's mum hadn't seen Baz at all, but she *was* in a bit of a dither. "Boys! Where have you been? Tom's bus has gone!"

"Sorry, Mum," said Coxie. "We went to Dr Pennyfather's place because Tom left something there. Can he stay the night?"

"If it's all right with his parents," said Coxie's mum.

I phoned home. Mum seemed really pleased that I wanted to stay. "You're having a good time, then?" she said. "What did you find out?"

"I'll tell you when I get home, Mum." I crossed my fingers, hard, because before I saw Mum again I might be travelling through time. I might be cured! Then again, perhaps I'd lost my chance. If Palmer's friends were after Baz, he might not have time to worry about my problems.

"I just hope Baz doesn't get caught," I said to Coxie while his mum was putting the Noise Machine to bed. "And I hope he's careful if he finds the medallions. If he takes them away before we used them, things might *un*happen."

"Maybe," said Coxie. He paused. "Then again, if we'd never gone time-travelling, if *that* unhappened, you wouldn't have been shot in the first place and you wouldn't have nerve-burn now."

I hadn't thought of that. Maybe Baz wouldn't need to take me into the future for a cure. Maybe he could arrange to have the nerve-burn unhappen instead.

"If he does, I won't be here," I said.

"I won't be here, either," said Coxie. "If it hadn't been for time-travelling, I would have kept going to the Adventurers. If I hadn't left, Wattsie wouldn't have come to see Mum about it and they wouldn't have married. The Noise Machine wouldn't have been born and... " He groaned. "The things you get me into!"

"Perhaps we could just undo what happened to me, and leave your life alone," I said.

"Baz will be doing the undoing, so he'll choose what he undoes," said Coxie. "There's something fishy about that man, Tom. He's in too much of a hurry. If there's anything time-travellers have plenty of, it's time. Why didn't he just go home and make you a TDD? He could have been back here in seconds. Or even less."

"Baz is all right," I said. "Don't forget, he has Palmer's gang after him."

"I hope he's all right, for your sake," said Coxie.

It's a horrible feeling, knowing you've got a disease from the future. It's also unpleasant to know you could suddenly lose nearly two years' worth of memories. Would we notice, if it happened? Or would we blink and find ourselves somewhere else?

It made me dizzy, just thinking about everything that would be affected if Baz undid two years. I suppose that's why I agreed to go to the movies with Coxie. His mum gave me the money for a ticket.

"I'll meet you outside the theatre when the film's over," she said.

"That's all right, Mum. We'll walk home," said Coxie. "It's only a few blocks."

"Tom? How do you feel about that?"

I felt dreadful, but I managed a weak grin. "I'm all right, Mrs Watts."

We were just about to leave when there was a phone call from Mum.

"Tom, have you done anything you shouldn't have done?" she asked.

"No," I said. "Why?"

"I've just had a strange call from the police," said Mum. "It seems Dr Pennyfather has lodged a complaint against you."

"Well! She was just as rude to me as I was to her! Even more!" I said.

"It's not about rudeness," said Mum. "That skull has been stolen, and Dr Pennyfather is blaming you."

"I didn't steal it!" I said. "I didn't even see it! The old bat just went for me, then practically threw me out of the gate."

"According to the police, she thinks you must have crept back later," said Mum.

"Well, I didn't."

"I didn't think you had." Mum sighed. "The police are coming to talk to you this evening. I'd better square it with Coxie's mum. If there's any real trouble, you let me know and Dad and I'll come straight away."

I handed the phone over to Coxie's mum.

"What was all that about?" asked Coxie.

"Lizba's skull's been stolen, and Dr Pennyfather thinks I did it. The police are coming here."

"Oh, great!" said Coxie. "Mum's going to love that!"

Coxie's mum wasn't too pleased, and I couldn't blame her. No one wants the police on their doorstep. It's bad for the family reputation.

"I didn't do it," I told her. "It's all a mistake."

"Of course," she said, but she kept giving me these doubtful little looks. And when Sergeant Kerry arrived he gave me the same look, too.

"You seemed extremely interested in this skull, Tom," he said.

"I still am," I said. "But if I'd been planning to take it, would I have been asking you about it?"

"Probably not," said Sergeant Kerry.

"When did it happen?" I asked. "I've been with Coxie most of the day, so maybe I have an alibi."

"That's the trouble," said Sergeant Kerry. "Since the alarms and security system were bypassed, the theft could have taken place anytime during the past three days or nights. Dr Pennyfather says she had no occasion to examine the skull until this evening. She went to verify a measurement, and found the skull had been removed from the storeroom."

"I'm sure Tom had nothing to do with it," said Coxie's mum. "He only arrived this morning and he's been with my son ever since."

Sergeant Kerry looked puzzled. "You haven't been to Dr Pennyfather's, Tom?"

"Only this morning," I said. "I went to find out what she was going to do with the skull."

"Did you see it?"

"I didn't even go into the house. She threw me out."

"How long were you there?"

"I got there about nine, and left soon after," I said.

"Can anyone verify the fact that you left her house straight away?"

"She can. And I went into a clothes shop in the mall. I thought someone was following me, so I told the assistant. The store detective stopped the man while I went out the back way. They'd both remember me."

Coxie's mum gawked at me. "Tom! I didn't know anything about this!" she said.

"It was just a mistake," I said. "It turned out the man was someone who knew me. At least, I knew his mother."

"And you haven't been back to Dr Pennyfather's house, today." Sergeant Kerry put away his notes. He obviously thought he was wasting his time.

"Coxie and I were outside her place at about half past three," I said. "We saw her let a visitor in."

"I see." Sergeant Kerry put on his hat. "That would have been Dr Smith. Dr Pennyfather mentioned him."

"What happens now?" I asked.

"I'm sure you have nothing to worry about, Tom. Since a sophisticated alarm system was bypassed in the theft, it seems unlikely that anyone your age could have been involved."

I know kids my age who can make electronic circuits sit up and beg, but I didn't say so. "Thanks," I said, instead.

"However," said Sergeant Kerry, "I'll give you some advice, Tom. Stay away from Dr Pennyfather's place."

"The boys were just off to the movies," said Coxie's mum. "Is that all right?"

"That's fine," said Sergeant Kerry. "You're sure this person who followed you is OK, Tom?"

"He's cool. Coxie and I were talking to him this afternoon," I said. "Can we go now? We don't want to miss the film."

"I'd offer a lift in the police car," said Sergeant Kerry, "but I'm not allowed to use it for innocent boys."

He laughed, and left, and Coxie and I went to the movies. The film had started, but we hadn't missed much.

During a slow part of the movie, Coxie decided to get some popcorn. I stayed put in my seat. I was dog-tired, so I thought I was dreaming when I saw Dr Pennyfather coming down the aisle.

Interview with the Old Bat

She was peering around, and arguing loudly with one of the ushers. Oh, no. The old bat was looking for me!

No normal anthropologist chases kids into movie theatres, but Dr Pennyfather wasn't a normal anthropologist. I thought about making a run for it, but that would make her think I was guilty. I scrunched down, but she came along the row and sat down beside me.

"That's my friend's seat," I said.

"Then let's discuss this in the lobby," she replied.

I didn't want to discuss it at all, but I followed her out. I looked around for Coxie, but he'd disappeared.

"What do you want?" I said. "I didn't take the skull, so there's no use hassling me."

Dr Pennyfather snorted. "This isn't about the skull, it's about the medallions."

"What medallions?"

"Don't pretend to be stupid, young man. When you forced your way on to my property this morning…"

"You let me in!" I said furiously.

"You had some metallic artefacts," she said, "that you very carelessly left on my lawn."

"I meant to put them back in my pocket."

"Tell me about them. Every detail."

"You weren't interested this morning," I said coldly. "You told me to get out."

"Listen, young man..."

"Stop calling me that," I said. "My name is Tom Stratton. And why should I help you? You threw me out, and you set the police on me. Now you're following me around. I didn't take the skull, and the medallions have nothing to do with you."

"If they are clues to the history of the skull, they are very much to do with me," said Dr Pennyfather. "And you obviously know something about them. Tell me."

"No," I said. "You wouldn't listen before. You wouldn't believe me, anyway. What was it you said this morning? That the only interest you had in *me* was in my absence? Well, I'm saying the same to you. If you want to see the film, go and watch it. If you don't, go home."

Dr Pennyfather's face was going red. She could dish it out, but she obviously couldn't take it! I saw her take a deep breath, and I knew she really wanted this information. "All right, Tom," she said. "I'm going to do you the favour of treating you like a fellow rational adult."

"Gee, *thanks*," I growled. I didn't think that was much of an honour. If Dr Pennyfather was a rational adult, I was King Kong.

"Tell me about Dr Smith."

"I don't know any Dr Smith."

75

"Of course you do," she said impatiently. "You left this for him."

She held out the note I'd left and I could have kicked myself. Imagine being stupid enough to sign my name and give Coxie's phone number. I'd never thought that *she* would get hold of it.

"You mean Baz," I said. "I don't know him well. I knew his mother."

"And his mother is the person who originally owned the medallions?"

"Right. They were damaged, and she left them with me about a year ago. I was going to show them to you, but you couldn't be bothered. Then Baz wanted them back. I told him I thought I'd dropped them at your place, so he went to get them."

Dr Pennyfather was staring at me.

"It's true," I said, exhausted. My hands were beginning to shake again.

"Very well. Where and when did Ms Smith give you the medallions? Where and when did you meet Ms Smith?"

"Who the heck is Ms Smith?"

"Dr Smith's mother," said Dr Pennyfather.

"Oh, I met her a year or so ago in the Asbestos Ranges, and she gave me the medallions the same day." (It wasn't the same day, of course. The days were hundreds of years apart, but there was no use telling Dr Pennyfather that.)

"Where and when did she first obtain them?" The old bat could teach Sergeant Kerry a thing or two about grilling suspects.

"She made them."

As soon as I'd said it, I knew I'd made a mistake. Dr Pennyfather knew, too. "How very odd," she said triumphantly. "Dr Smith believes the artefacts to be several centuries old. His mother must have been an extremely venerable lady, or an untruthful one."

I shrugged. "That's what she told me," I said. "You're the expert. What do *you* think?"

"I think you know far more than you're telling me, Tom Stratton."

"Why didn't you examine them when you had them?" I asked.

She frowned. "Dr Smith left rather suddenly," she said, and for the first time she sounded a bit uncertain.

Wow! Baz must have flicked back (or forward) in time and practically vanished right in front of her. No wonder she was interested! No wonder she'd bothered to find me!

"Have you known Dr Smith for long?"

"I never met the man before today, all right? His mum left the medallions with me. He wanted them back. I told him I must have dropped them at your place this morning. I didn't want to tangle with you again, so I sent him to get them himself. He obviously did. End of story."

"You don't have his home address? Or a contact number where I can reach him?"

"I want to see the film," I said, trying not to sway. "Goodbye, Doctor."

Dr Pennyfather dug in her pocket for a notebook and pencil and scribbled down some numbers. She ripped out the page and held it out to me. "If Dr Smith contacts you, or if you remember anything more about him, phone me at this number," she said. "It's very important."

I considered tearing up the phone number and scattering it around the lobby, but that would have made me a litter-lout, so I just shoved it in my pocket and went back into the theatre. I didn't look back.

The film was good, I suppose, but I couldn't really concentrate. I was much too busy thinking. No wonder Dr Pennyfather was interested if Baz had disappeared right in front of her! I wondered what she really thought about the medallions. They were melted, and I didn't think she could have guessed they were from the future. Anyway, Baz had them now. And Baz had gone off with them, somewhere in time, evading Palmer's friends. Baz was trying to find the medallions in working condition. He could be anywhere in any year. He might decide not to come back at all.

I shivered. If Baz didn't come back, I didn't have much hope for my chances.

I'd really overdone it that day, and when the film ended, I was exhausted. The thought of walking back to Coxie's place made me wilt, but I couldn't bring myself to call his mum and ask for a lift. I'd already caused her enough trouble.

I hoped some of Coxie's friends might offer to give us a ride back. I could pretend I had twisted my ankle or something. "See anyone you know, Coxie?" I asked.

"No," said Coxie. "What happened to you during the film?"

"I was being grilled by the old bat," I said, "Dr Pennyfather. She thinks there's something very weird about Baz."

"Well, there *is*," said Coxie. "Wait a minute! Do you mean she came in *here*?"

"Yes. She was asking a lot of questions about Baz and the medallions."

We were walking slowly, and just about everyone else had gone. The next thing I knew, two people appeared from behind us. They split up so they were walking on either side of us. "Tom Stratton?" said the man.

"What?" I stopped and looked sideways.

"Are you Tom Stratton?"

"Yes. Hey! Get your hands off me!" The man had taken a firm hold of my elbow, and I could see Coxie was being held in an armlock by the woman.

"Be quiet," said the man. "We need to talk to you."

"If you don't let me go, I'll scream," I said.

"Calm down," said the woman. "We won't hurt you."

"Let go!" said Coxie.

"You're coming with us," said the man. He sounded so much like a cop in a bad thriller that I almost laughed.

"Why should we?" I asked.

"Because you must. You have become involved in a situation that should never have arisen. You may have information that can be of great assistance to us. You must return the sol-shot, and also the time medallions."

"You've been watching too much television," I said. I was shaking, but I tried to sound bored. "Coxie and I don't know what you're talking about."

The man glanced at his partner, and they both reached for their belts.

"Stop!" said Coxie.

Somehow, he'd pulled the sol-shot out of his pocket, and he was pointing it at the woman. She let him go and backed away. I didn't blame her. I'd seen what a sol-shot could do.

"Let Tom go," said Coxie. His voice was shaking, but he wasn't running out on me.

The man let go of my arm. "You really must come with us," he said. "It's for your own good."

"Must nothing!" said Coxie. "If you're Palmer's friends, we don't have to do anything for you. You've got no right messing up our lives! Come on, Tom."

We backed away. Coxie kept the sol-shot in his hand. I knew the safety-button was still on, but they didn't.

Coxie ducked around a corner, and dragged me after him. "Let's go to the mall," hissed Coxie, "and take a short cut home."

We heard footsteps coming, then suddenly they stopped. I glanced back, just in time to see the man and woman vanish.

The Choice

"They've gone," I said, and flopped down, breathing hard.

"But where," said Coxie. "And *when?*"

We soon found out, because the pair popped into view ahead of us. While they were getting their bearings, we ducked behind the fountain where we had met Baz earlier that day.

It's creepy being chased by time-travellers. They can pop in and out, and appear where you least expect them. You're not safe from time-travellers anywhere. We couldn't even go to Coxie's house and lock ourselves in. A time-traveller only had to come to Coxie's front door, go back a few hundred years, take four or five steps forward, come back to the present, and be inside the house.

I think the chase lasted about twenty minutes; it seemed like two days. I think they would have caught us, eventually, but then Coxie backed right into Baz, who'd appeared behind us. I think Baz was as surprised as we were, because he was tapping the TDD on his wrist when I looked around. He soon took in what was happening, though. "Looks like you boys need some help," he said. Baz snaked his arm around Coxie and took the sol-shot. "My, where did you get *this*?" he asked, turning it over, but keeping his eye on the other time-travellers.

"It was Lizba's," I gasped.

"What luck!" said Baz cheerfully. "Sit down, Tom, while I send this pair on their way."

I sat down.

"Really, James," said Baz to the other man. "I thought you would have more sense. Were you trying to abduct these two lads? That hardly fits in with your high ideals."

The man called James ignored him. "It is imperative that you come with us, Tom," he said. He still sounded like a bad actor pretending to be a police officer. "Don't trust this man. He's a wanted criminal, and he's meddling with things he doesn't understand. Besides that, you are in a very serious situation. You have an illness that…"

"I've got nerve-burn," I said. "I know. You didn't have to grab me to tell me that."

"We can offer treatment, if you agree to our terms," said the woman.

"Yeah. So can Baz. And there are no terms with Baz. I helped him, he'll help me."

James turned to the woman. "I told you, Maria. We should have stunned them first."

"We had to verify their identity," she said.

"How many cases of nerve-burn could there be in the twentieth century?"

She shrugged. "We really couldn't even be certain it *was* nerve-burn."

"It seems certain now," said James. "Look how pale he is. We're just in time."

"If I *do* have it, it's Palmer's fault!" I snapped. "He shot me."

"Palmer?" said Maria quickly. "Palmer shot you?"

"Well, I didn't give the nerve-burn to myself."

"A blast of active power wouldn't cause any real lasting damage," said Maria. "We had assumed long-term exposure to an exhausted…"

"Well, this *has* been a lovely chat," interrupted Baz. "Tom, I've traced the working medallions. Are you ready to go and collect them?"

I looked at Baz and then at James and Maria. "What about Coxie?" I asked.

"We don't need Coxie," said Baz. "Come on. I can have you back in a second or two."

I didn't really want to go on my own with Baz. "Come on, Coxie," I said.

"No, *you* come on," said Coxie. "Let's go home and let them sort themselves out. They're all after something."

"No, Tom, please come over here," said Maria. "You must trust us."

"Yes," said Baz. "He's really going to trust a couple of kidnappers whose friend shot him."

"That's ridiculous," said Maria. "Tom, this man means nothing but trouble. He's a thief and a…"

"Tom, have I ever tried to make you do anything you didn't want to do?" asked Baz.

I'd had enough. They were arguing over me as if I were a piece of meat. "I wish you'd all leave us alone," I said. "We don't owe any of you anything. If you won't help me, go away."

There was a little silence after that, and then we heard a tapping of heels. I looked around and there was the old bat herself, Dr Pennyfather. I think I groaned.

"Dr Smith," said Dr Pennyfather. "I have very good reason to believe you have not been completely honest with me. I must insist that you explain how it was that you were able…"

"Yes, you explain it to her," I said to Baz. "I'm going."

I turned away, but Baz put his hand on my shoulder, and Coxie and the others disappeared.

It wasn't like time-travelling with the medallions. I felt as if I'd left my stomach behind, and everything looked wrong. We were still in the mall, and it was still dark, but somehow it just felt all wrong. The mall seemed to flicker, then steadied.

I let out a yell, and then I doubled over. I felt really sick. "What's going on, Baz?" I croaked. "I said I didn't want to come."

"Never mind that now," said Baz. "We've got to get to Dr Pennyfather's place."

There was another flicker, and he tapped the TDD.

"Why?" I said. "If you wanted to see her, she was just there. And you've already got the medallions."

Baz laughed. "I also have the sol-shot." He tossed up the ray gun and caught it. "Now all I need is the skull and I've got all the proof I need of Lizba's fate."

"The skull's been stolen," I muttered. "Remember? And I bet you did it."

"Not yet," said Baz. "I haven't stolen it yet."

"Someone has. Sergeant Kerry and Dr Pennyfather said so."

"They're not important. Come on, Tom." He grabbed my arm and pulled me upright.

"Leave me alone," I said. "I want to rest."

"You can rest all you want in a month or so," said Baz cheerfully. "It's lucky I found you in time. Another few weeks and I'd have been too late." He laughed again. "That is, I would have had to go away and come back earlier."

He hurried me through the mall. At one point my legs gave way, but that didn't stop Baz. He just bent down and threw me across his shoulders. After a short time we were outside Dr Pennyfather's place.

"Right," said Baz, putting me down. "Let's get to that skull. I need to verify its identity."

"It's not there," I said. "I told you."

"Tom, Tom, you are so very literal! Now listen. This is two nights ago from your perspective. Dr Pennyfather is currently enjoying a dinner out with a Dr Kane."

"You're crazy!" I said. "Those alarms will go off the second you try to get in, and you'll have the police on us!"

Baz thought that was very funny. "No, Tom."

"The security cameras will pick us up."

"No, they won't."

"Those other people will catch you."

"Not while I have you as a hostage. How many paces do you think it would take to reach the house from here?"

"I don't know and I don't care." I wanted to get away from Baz, but I couldn't run, and besides, he'd brought me back in time. Only a couple of days back, but I couldn't stay here. I'd be in two places at once.

"You'd *better* care," said Baz.

"Why?"

"If we get it wrong you might find yourself suddenly materializing inside a wall."

A Theft in Time

"Fortunately, I don't leave these things to chance," said Baz, when he thought I'd suffered enough. "We will need thirteen paces to the house and three more to clear the interior walls."

There was another flicker, and my stomach dropped again. I struggled not to be sick.

"What's *wrong* with that thing?" I gasped.

"I don't know," said Baz. "It doesn't seem to work the way it should."

"You ought to know. You said you made it."

"I lied," said Baz smugly.

We were standing among trees. "Sixteen paces," said Baz. "Will you walk, or do I carry you?"

"You can carry me," I said sourly. "Then I won't end up in any walls. You're a creep, Baz. You don't care about me at all. Not like Lizba did."

"Did Lizba care about you when she let you get shot?" He still sounded amused.

I didn't want to think about that at the moment. "*When* are we now?"

"About AD 1700, give or take a decade." Baz paced out the distance, there was another flicker, and we were standing in a dimly lit hallway. My stomach couldn't take much more of this. Neither could I.

"Here we are," said Baz. "Right back where we were." He laughed.

There were some really ugly wooden masks on the walls, but I didn't have time to stare. Baz dragged me along the hallway and made me open a door. "In here, I think," he said.

It was a storage room, full of jars and boxes and crates. "Open the boxes," said Baz. He had the sol-shot in his hand, and now he wasn't smiling any more. I did as he said. It was very hard work; my hands were numb and almost useless.

"Why do you need me?" I asked.

"You're a hostage to keep James and Maria away," said Baz. "I also need you to help identify the skull."

The boxes were full of bones, bits of china, and so on. It would have been interesting if I hadn't been sick and terrified. By now I'd realized that Baz was going to make me steal the skull for him. After that, he'd just disappear and leave me to manage as best I could.

Lizba's skull was in the fourth box I opened. I stood looking down at it for a moment, then I went on to open another box. "Have you found it?" asked Baz.

I lifted out a skull from the box I'd just opened. It was brownish and broken. "This could be it."

Baz took it and looked at it closely. Then he smiled at me. "This is the skull of the selfless Lizba Smith?"

"It might be."

Baz put the skull back in the box. "Nice try, Tom. Now find the right one. Don't bother trying to bluff me again. I have the measurements from Lizba Smith's file."

"She wasn't your mother, was she?" I said. I opened another box. I was playing for time, but I don't know why I bothered.

"What makes you think that?" said Baz.

"You don't care about her at all. And now I think I remember where I've seen you before."

"Really?" He didn't seem too worried.

"You were present in Lizba's lab when I wrecked the computer. You were one of Palmer's gang, weren't you?"

He didn't answer.

"So that means James and Maria are on the other side. I should have gone with them. Who are they, anyway? Friends of Lizba's?"

Baz grinned. "They never met Lizba Smith. They're meddlers from the future. *My* future. Oh, they have very high-sounding ideals about clearing up anomalies in the past, but when you come down to it, they're no better than I am. If they think time-travel is so bad, what are they doing with these?" And he waved his TDD at me.

"Why do you really want the skull?" I asked. "And why did you really want the medallions? You're not still trying to kill Kane?"

"I never cared all that much about Kane," said Baz. "I need the skull simply to prove that Lizba Smith is dead. Since there were no reliable witnesses, and Lizba was as sly as they come, I suspected she had simply moved forward in time. That meant she could turn up any year, or could even be behind the activities of the wonderful James and Maria. I *know* Palmer is dead, but the whereabouts of Lizba has always been a mystery. Without proof she's dead, I can't be sure she won't pop up to bother me again.

"In a way, I was hoping she might be alive. It would have been interesting to talk to her, and with you as a hostage I could very well have persuaded her to give me the medallions."

"You have time-travel yourself," I said. "You said you developed it from Lizba's notes! You could go to her in her past if you're that keen."

"I tried to develop time-travel from an early version of Palmer's notes," corrected Baz. "But, they're incomplete, and I haven't been very successful."

"What about that?" I pointed to the TDD on his arm. "That seems to work."

"This isn't mine," said Baz. "I took it from James. A neat trick, right? James comes zipping back through the years, trying to stop my little experiments, and I knocked him out with a sol-shot and removed his TDD. The only problem is, these things aren't very reliable, particularly when they're used to translate two people at once. They really *are* designed for solo use, and this one could go wrong at any time. In fact, it's flicked me back to my own time quite often." He smiled again. "Nice thought, isn't it, Tom? Every translation could be my last and I'd be stuck at home. Or possibly here in the twentieth century. That really would be an anomaly. Now, get that skull and then tell me exactly when and where I can find the medallions in good working order."

Baz was getting impatient, so I went back and picked up Lizba's skull. I'd forgotten how beautiful it was, a pearly blue-green colour. "This is it," I said.

Baz took it casually. "Yes, so it is. I recognize the contours. Then Lizba Smith really is dead." He shook his head. "She probably wouldn't have helped me anyway."

Baz made me replace the boxes, then we left. There was another flicker. I felt... well, I felt like dying.

"Where... I mean, *when* are we now?" I asked wearily.

"This is the same time we left from the mall. Now for the medallions," reminded Baz. "Where and when can I easily obtain them, Tom?"

I groaned. "I can't think," I said. "It's ages ago."

"You'd better think, for your own sake," said Baz. He sounded quite pleasant, but I could imagine what he might do if I didn't help. On the other hand, I couldn't let him take the medallions out of my past. He might undo Coxie's life and mess up mine even more. Besides, would *you* let a character like Baz loose with time medallions?

So, while I pretended to think about how Baz could get the medallions, I actually thought about how to stop him.

First, I considered sending Baz to the Asbestos Ranges, to the day before Coxie and I found the skull. His chances of locating the medallions there were pretty slim. Then I realized he'd take me with him, and I didn't feel well enough to climb hills.

Next, I tried to remember where they really *had* been. Mostly in my bedroom at home. And, at one time, Coxie and I had each had one. Coxie had never liked the medallions much. He'd wanted them both at one time, but only to stop me from using them...

"I've remembered," I said.

"Where and when?" said Baz.

"Coxie had the medallions in his dresser about a year and a half ago. If you pick the first Wednesday in May, at about noon, there'll be no one home."

"You wouldn't lie to me, Tom?"

"Listen," I said. "I don't care what happens in your time. Why should I? Shall I fetch the medallions myself? I know where he kept them." I hoped Baz wouldn't want to chance me using them and I was right.

"Goodbye, Tom," he said.

"Wait!" I said. "What about my nerve-burn? Are you coming back?"

"I doubt it," said Baz. "I'd cure you if I could, but that's impossible."

"But in your time…" I began.

"There's no cure in my time either," said Baz. "Your best chance is to go back to James and Maria, if they're still at the mall. They're from my future; maybe they can help."

"Thanks a lot," I said bitterly. But I was talking to the empty air.

Nerve-Burn

"Great," I muttered. "Just great."

I had sent Baz off on a wild-goose chase, because Coxie had never had the time medallions at his place in Devonport. Eighteen months ago he'd lived near me. I wondered what would happen. Baz would go to the place where Coxie lived now. Either there would be no one at home and Baz would search and wouldn't find anything, or else there *would* be someone home. If so, I hoped they would call the police. The police would never catch Baz, but they might hold him up for awhile and give me a chance to find the others. But, Baz could spend a year in the past and still pop up right now in my present. And he wouldn't be a happy time-traveller when he did.

All I had was the time it would take him to walk to Coxie's house and back again, so I knew I'd better get to the mall. I just hoped James and Maria would still be there. I forced myself to walk. One foot in front of the other, one, two, one, two. As I started along the footpath, I hoped James and Maria had got rid of Dr Pennyfather. I didn't think I could face more of her questions, particularly if she started going on about the skull. There was another thing; my fingerprints would be all over her storeroom now!

I wondered how I'd explain that to Sergeant Kerry and Mum and Dad, then I started getting a funny feeling that I'd never have to explain anything to any of them. All of a sudden, I couldn't feel my feet.

I looked down to see what was going on, but that was a mistake. The ground seemed to be heaving under me. I jerked upright and forced myself to keep going.

I'd got about halfway to the mall before I collapsed. One minute I was staggering along the footpath, the next I saw the path coming towards me and I was flat on my face. When I tried to get up, I realized I couldn't move.

It wasn't like the time Palmer had shot me. Then I'd been paralyzed. This time, I wasn't numb and I wasn't paralyzed. I could feel every bump and bruise and they all hurt a lot. I remember pawing at the footpath, trying to push myself upright, and wondering vaguely why nothing was happening. That was when I realized I simply hadn't the strength to get up.

I think that's when it really hit me that I was going to die right there. I'd been trying to get to Maria and James, counting on a cure, but now it was too late. I could feel my life draining away, and I was shocked because it had all been so sudden. Back in the mall I'd been feeling bad, but not all that much worse than I'd felt for months. Now I felt about fifty times worse. It must have been all that zipping about in time.

I tried to tell myself Coxie and James and Maria would find me soon, but I didn't really believe it. They didn't know where I was and they didn't know when I was. For all they knew, Baz could have whisked me off to another century.

That's when I heard jogging footsteps. I couldn't see who it was, but somehow I knew it was Coxie, and that he'd seen me. "Are you all right, Tom?" he said.

I think I made a sort of gurgle.

"It's all right, they've gone," said Coxie. "I managed to persuade them that they didn't need us after all." He laughed. "I figure Dr Pennyfather had a bit to do with that! She wanted their names and addresses and everything. I think they were glad to get away from her. Of course they had to walk around the corner before they left. It's bad enough that she saw Baz zip out. If she'd seen James and Maria do it, too, she'd have flipped her lid."

"How did you find me?" I muttered.

"I figured that Baz would go back a couple of days and steal the skull, so that meant you had to be near Dr Pennyfather's place. Was I right, or was I right?" Coxie sounded awfully pleased with himself.

"He's got the sol-shot and he's gone looking for the medallions," I mumbled.

"Good riddance," said Coxie. "James and Maria will catch up with him before he does anything else. They don't approve of people from the future coming back here."

"*They* came back."

"That was only to catch Baz and to clear up a few anomalies. It's over now, for us, so get up. Mum'll be wondering what's taking us so long."

"I can't get up, Coxie," I said. "I've got nerve-burn, remember? And now you've sent James and Maria away, so I'm going to die. You didn't think of that, did you?"

There was a brief silence. I could only see Coxie's feet and ankles, but I could imagine the look on his face. He might be bigger and stronger now, but he was still the same old Coxie, and I knew I'd hurt his feelings. "I thought you wanted them to go," he said finally.

"I'm going to die," I said again.

Coxie squatted and put his hand on my shoulder. "You can't get nerve-burn from being shot by one of those guns," he said. "Maria said the effect is only temporary."

"But Baz said... Oh, forget it." I knew I couldn't depend on anything Baz had said. "Fine," I muttered. "So how long is this temporary effect going to last?" My voice was slurring.

My hands and feet were numb now, and the backs of my legs were cold. I couldn't feel my face any more, and soon I wouldn't be able to speak. I could hear Coxie saying something, and I thought how weird it was that I couldn't quite follow what he was saying.

Then I thought how weird it was altogether that Tom Stratton, who'd been time-travelling through the centuries, should die right here, and right now. If it had to happen at all, I'd rather die at home, or get killed fighting dinosaurs or monsters. Or maybe I'd rather die like Lizba, fighting to save the future world. Only Lizba's death hadn't really achieved anything, had it? Time-travel still existed, and now that Baz knew for certain she was dead, who knew what he would do. Then I thought it wouldn't make any difference to me. Nothing would make any difference to me, now.

What made it all even worse was when Dr Pennyfather came tapping up beside us. "What does he think he's doing?" Dr Pennyfather asked Coxie loudly. "What's wrong with him?"

Timedetectors

Dr Pennyfather sounded pretty mad, and it felt like she actually poked me with her toe. What sort of person pokes a dying kid with her toe? A Dr Pennyfather sort of person. But, then, perhaps Dr Pennyfather didn't really mean to be an old bat. She was just so interested in studying historical humans, that she had lost touch with how to deal with the living ones.

Another thing about Dr Pennyfather; she was *not* stupid. And she had the courage of her convictions. She'd seen Baz and me disappear, and she'd seen Maria and James and Lizba's skull. She knew none of those things fit in with normal life in the twentieth century and she wanted to know more. Any normal person would have decided she was seeing things and gone to an eye doctor or a shrink. Not Dr Pennyfather. She knew she was right.

Dr Pennyfather prodded me again and demanded that I sit up and answer questions. "What happened to you?" she said. "Where is Dr Smith?"

When I didn't answer, she crouched down. "Is he hurt?" she asked Coxie. "Did you see him fall?"

"He was like this when I got here," said Coxie.

"He seems to have had some sort of seizure," Dr Pennyfather muttered. I don't think she was worried about me. She just wanted to question me about Baz.

"He hasn't been very well," said Coxie. "I think we should get him home."

Dr Pennyfather rolled me over and poked my neck. "That's odd," she said. "There seems to be some sort of muscle spasm. Tom, what happened? Do you have any allergies? Did you hurt yourself?"

I gasped. At this point I was having serious trouble breathing.

"I suppose I should call an ambulance," Dr Pennyfather sighed, pulling out her mobile phone. I don't know what she said, but there wasn't much of a wait before the ambulance came blazing down the street.

I remember seeing the red light and hearing the noise, then suddenly people were grabbing me and Dr Pennyfather was explaining and Coxie was looking increasingly worried. Then I stopped breathing.

It's hard to describe what happened next. Have you ever listened to a radio that isn't tuned properly? Sometimes you hear two people talking at once, and the voices overlap. It was like that. I heard someone in the ambulance say: "We're losing him," and at the same time, I heard someone else say: "We've got him."

Then the lights went out. When they came back on, I was lying in a sort of tent, and there was red light all around me. Something very cold hit my neck, and I passed out again.

The next time I woke up, the red light had gone. So had the tent. I was still in bed, but this time I was covered with a sheet and I felt normal. I sat up, and found my muscles had come back to life. *That* was a real relief, so I flopped back down and thought about it.

I'm in hospital, I decided. Then I wondered where Mum and Dad were. And where was Coxie? I heard footsteps and I started to calm down. I even closed my eyes.

"You're awake." That's what people always say on television when someone's in hospital, so of course I said, "No, I'm still asleep." I wasn't trying to be funny, it was just a reflex.

"You *are* awake," said the voice, and I groaned. It was Dr Pennyfather.

"Look," I said, "I've had a horrible experience, and I don't want another one just yet. I want Mum and Dad. Where are they?"

Dr Pennyfather loomed over me, so I sat up again.

"Never mind them," she said. "They're not here, and this is more important. How are you feeling?"

I gaped at her. I never thought Dr Pennyfather would care about my health. Then I found out she *didn't* care. All she wanted was to find out what it felt like to be irradiated with red rays. She had a notebook and a pencil, and she started grilling me.

"What do you remember? Did the red rays feel hot? Is your skin tender? Abnormally sensitive? Numb?"

"Look," I said finally, "are you a doctor? A doctor of medicine, I mean?"

"I am an anthropologist."

"But are you a doctor of medicine?"

"No."

"In that case, my health has nothing to do with you and you can put that notebook away," I said. Then I remembered that she'd called the ambulance. "It's not that I'm ungrateful," I added.

Dr Pennyfather's eyes gleamed. "Then you can demonstrate your gratitude by answering my questions."

She had a point, so I answered what I could, then she started poking at the equipment. That made me a bit nervous, because some of the equipment was connected to the bed – and *me*.

"Look, I wish you'd stop that," I said. She was still nosing around when Coxie came in, followed by James and Maria.

Call me stupid if you want, but it wasn't until then that I realized I wasn't in the local hospital. Well, how was I to know I'd been hauled into the future? Hospitals look and smell the same in the thirty-fifth century as they do in the twentieth century.

Coxie sat down by the bed. "That was close," he said. "Listen, the timedetectors want to talk to us. Do you feel up to it?"

"Timedetectors?"

"James and Maria. They're police from the Kane Foundation. Temporal investigators, is what they call themselves. I call them timedetectors."

"The Kane Foundation? What's that?"

"Remember that man Kane that Lizba thought was so important?" said Coxie. "The one that Palmer wanted to kidnap and probably kill before he grew up? Well, Kane survived, and after Palmer's gang was disbanded he thought everything was all right. Then one of them started messing around with time-travel again."

"That'd be Baz," I said.

"Yes. He wasn't too successful, and there was really nothing anyone could pin on him, but Kane thought there might be trouble later. He started the Kane Foundation to develop time-travel properly, then he had the technology locked away. He set up a task force to sort through history to find anomalies that indicated time-travellers had been interfering when and where they shouldn't. It's James and Maria's job to go back and set things right."

"How? By grabbing people like us?" I said.

"Hey, don't knock it!" said Coxie. "If they hadn't grabbed you, you'd be history."

Anomaly

"I *am* history if we're in the future," I said. "And so are you. What year is this?"

Coxie shrugged. "We're some time in the thirty-fifth or thirty-sixth century, I think. They won't tell us any more than that. That really upsets Dr Pennyfather!"

"I bet," I said. "What's she doing here, anyway?"

Coxie winked at me. "James calls her an 'unavoidable complication'. I like James."

"Hmm," I said. I didn't feel like liking anyone just then, not even Coxie.

"So," I said to James. "I can see why you wanted to get Baz if he stole your TDD, but what do Coxie and I have to do with it?"

James glanced irritably at Dr Pennyfather. "I think you should leave."

"I am not going anywhere," said Dr Pennyfather. "You have kept me confined in this building for a week without answers, and now I demand my rights."

"Oh, let her stay, James," said Maria wearily. "It won't make any difference. Tom is the important one right now. And the major problem." She looked at me, and there was something in her eyes that worried me. The vet had had a look like that when our old dog had broken his leg.

"If I'm a problem, it's Palmer's fault, not mine," I said. "What's wrong with me?"

"Nothing," said Maria. She smiled. It was the first time I'd seen her look anything but bothered or bored, and I saw Coxie give her an admiring sideways look.

"What do you mean, nothing wrong with me?" I said. "I almost died back there! Maybe I *did* die back there! You don't die from nothing."

"Believe me, Tom," said Maria, "there is nothing wrong with you, now. As a matter of fact, you don't need these any more." She removed the tubes from my arms. "You did have an extremely advanced case of nerve-burn, but your nerves and muscles seem to have satisfactorily regen…"

"Erhm!" said James. "He doesn't need to know that. Neither does *she*." (No prizes for knowing who he meant!)

Maria smiled again. "James is right. All you need to know is that the nerve-burn has been cured."

"How do you know? You said I couldn't have got it from being shot," I reminded her.

"The treatment," interrupted Dr Pennyfather, "I demand to know the treatment for this condition. The red spectra in the tent seemed to indicate the presence of some kind of radiation. Is that correct?"

James gave her a dirty look, but otherwise ignored her.

"The damage wasn't done by the original burst from the sol-shot," said Maria, seriously. "Nerve-burn occurs from long-term exposure to a sol-shot with an exhausted solar pack. It was designed to recharge itself from solar radiation. Do you understand?"

I nodded. "We have solar panels and solar calculators."

"If deprived of solar radiation," continued Maria, "a sol-shot will feed off any available source of power – in this case, you!"

"Ugh!" said Coxie. "Like a vampire!"

"You might say that," said Maria. "It was designed as an emergency measure, but occasionally it backfires."

"Long-term exposure…" I said. "I kept the thing in a box under my bed. Would that have caused the problem?"

"It certainly would," said Maria.

"So it was my own fault…" That meant it hadn't been Lizba's fault after all! It would never have occurred to her that I'd keep the thing under my bed! "I'd have got better then, once the sol-shot was properly recharged by the sun?" I asked.

"No," said Maria. "The damage was too far advanced. You died. In fact, it was the report on your death that alerted us to the anomaly."

109

"What do you mean, I died? I'm alive, aren't I?"

"During our research, we discovered an account of the death of a child from a mystery condition. It seemed quite likely that it was nerve-burn," said Maria. "That fact pointed to temporal anomaly, because the first reported case of nerve-burn didn't occur until 3151, not long after the sol-shot was developed. We decided to investigate, and during our research into your death, we found a few other anomalies; the presence of a skull from the thirty-second century and the report of a theft that seemed to point to the presence of a time-traveller."

"Baz."

"Yes, *Baz.*" Maria glanced at James. "Your condition led us to his activities. We traced the skull in question to the thirty-second century, to the period when the Kane Foundation was being set up. We translated back to that time and encountered Baz, who was engaged in secret temporal experiments. Unfortunately, we underestimated his investigating abilities."

"You certainly did, didn't you?" I said. "He stole one of your TDDs."

"We'll get it back from him," said James.

"That doesn't really matter, does it?" I said. "Baz said it didn't work properly. He'll probably get stuck sometime and you can go and get him."

James cleared his throat. "That TDD is in perfect working order. It is also self-energizing, somewhat like a sol-shot deprived of sunlight."

"It certainly made me feel bad," I said. "And Baz couldn't control it properly."

"Our TDDs work by converting human energy," said Maria. "Proper training is necessary to stabilize them. No doubt Baz allowed it to convert your energy as well as his own."

"And I didn't have much to convert," I said sourly.

"So," said Maria. "We have to find Baz and get that TDD or we could have multiple anomalies."

"You'll have your work cut out," I said. "He's hopping about collecting memorabilia. Or so he said."

Maria sighed. "We'll have to start our research all over again. Since we removed you from your critical period, the time-scheme has probably been changed."

"Why didn't you just let me die?" I asked.

"It was a matter of deciding which anomaly was less injurious," said Maria. "A death from nerve-burn before that condition should have been possible was only a minor factor, but the implications could have been large."

They certainly would have been large to me!

"I guess you could always go back and catch Baz in the mall," I said.

"Unfortunately, that would undo your recovery," said Maria. "No, if we decide to replace you in your own time-scheme, dead or alive, we'll have to try to intercept Baz at a later period."

The Other Option

"Dead or alive? *If* you decide to return me?"

"Please understand, Tom," said Maria, "if it were up to us, we'd take you home and consider it a job well done. But there are things that cannot be justified. The Kane Foundation exists to solve anomalies but some things, though regrettable, are the products of their times and can't be changed."

"Like what?" I said.

"Like the extinction of *Cacatua galerita*," said James grumpily. "That *could* be changed, if I were authorized to fetch some fresh DNA from the past, but will the Foundation allow it? No! They keep on citing natural causes!" He glowered at me. "I don't call it natural that people from your time and beyond destroyed the habitats of so many…"

"James." Maria warned.

Then Coxie spoke up. "*Cacatua galerita* is what Cracker is. Do you really mean there are no sulphur-crested cockatoos left? None at all?"

"None," said James crossly. "And of course all organic museum specimens had to be destroyed during the germ-purge of 3273. If I could get access to some fresh DNA, or even a feather, I could clone…"

"Stop it, James," said Maria. "In your case, Tom, no one could claim natural causes. Not when you were exposed to a danger from the future. I believe your death could be classified as anomalous to a high degree. The fact remains that if we reinsert you in your time-scheme, we could create more anomalies. We must identify all implications before we decide."

"What if you can't put me back?" I said.

"We would offer you a permanent home with us," said Maria.

"I want to go home."

"Believe me, Tom," said Maria, "we'd like to solve all the problems of the ages, but it can't be done. Our only job is to solve the anomalies brought about by the existence of time-travel, and to do it with the least possible disturbance to the fabric of time."

"You'd better stop Baz, then," I said. "It's your fault he's got the TDD."

Maria glanced at James. "It could be argued that the whole loop involving Baz is a recent anomaly," she said.

"We might not have found that without Tom. And since James and I intercepted you, Tom, we bear responsibility for any consequences. However, it still might be best if you remain with us."

There was a brief silence. "How about Coxie and Dr Pennyfather?" I asked.

"There's no problem with returning them to their own time-scheme," said Maria. "Subject to a thorough debriefing, of course."

Coxie looked relieved, but that didn't help me.

"Listen," I said. "I think I have a deal for you."

"Tom, it isn't ethical to bargain with the future," said Maria.

"Ethical or not, I have a plan," I said. "How's this? Baz is a much worse danger than I'd ever be. He has Lizba's time medallions, but they won't work. He also has Lizba's skull, the TDD, and the sol-shot. At this moment, he's on his way to get the medallions from the time when they were still working."

"He could have gone to any time period, though," objected Coxie. "To Lizba's, or ours, or any time before."

"I know where and when he is," I said. "Baz took me with him to steal the skull and made me tell him where and when to get the medallions. He could have dumped me anywhere in time, so I told him what he wanted to know."

Maria groaned.

"But," I said, "I told him the wrong time and the wrong place. So if you want to catch up with him, you've only got to arrange to be there a few minutes before he is."

"When and where?" demanded Maria. She was young and pretty, but for a moment she reminded me of Dr Pennyfather. Well, I'd learned a thing or two about dealing with bullies.

"This is where the deal comes in." I tried to sound firm, but my voice was shaking. "If I tell you, you've got a short cut to cleaning up the whole mess. But *if* I tell you, you've got to put me back – with Coxie – cured, and no questions asked. We won't say anything about time-travel or about you or your times. You know you can trust us! We kept Lizba's secret for more than a year."

Maria and James glanced at one another, then Maria nodded, slowly. "That sounds fair," she said. "In fact, you have the makings of a real temporal investigator, Tom! Are you sure you don't want to join us?"

"I'm sure," I said. "There's just one other thing. What happens to Baz when you catch him?"

"We return him to his own time-scheme," said Maria. "Having first removed his stolen TDD, naturally."

"And that's it?" I said.

"We have no authority to punish him."

"Great!" I said. "You talk about making *me* stay in the future, but you can't punish Baz! That's just not good enough. Baz will be up to something else as soon as your backs are turned, and I don't want to spend the rest of my life – now I've got a rest of my life – watching my back."

"What do you suggest, Tom?" asked Maria politely.

"I'll tell you when you get him," I said.

Maria smiled. "It's a deal. You tell us when and where to apprehend Baz."

I told them.

They took Coxie and me along, but they left Dr Pennyfather in the isolation zone of the Kane Foundation. Boy, was she mad! The whole operation went like a dream, especially for me. I can't tell you how good it felt to be healthy again! We went back to the date and place I'd given Baz, but an hour earlier. Maria and James got us into the house. (Since it was a weekday, no one was home.) James planted a pair of fake medallions in a dresser and, then, we waited.

Baz showed up, and found the medallions. While he was busy gloating, Maria hit him with a short blast from a sol-shot. Baz crumpled like a wet tissue, James got his TDD back, and we all went back to the Kane Foundation.

Baz was not a happy time-traveller, and pretty soon he wasn't a time-traveller at all.

"What happens to me now?" Baz asked, more or less the way I had.

"You should be debriefed and returned to your own time," said Maria. "However, I believe Tom has some ideas for your future, so we'll listen to him first."

Baz looked at me with a big grin, but I could tell he was uneasy.

"You ought to recruit him," I said. "Make him one of your research experts. He's good at finding things out, aren't you, Baz? Of course, he'd have to be based at the Foundation all the time."

They couldn't do it just like that. They had to check their records to find out what Baz had been doing in his own future. It turned out he'd disappeared soon after Lizba and Palmer had, so Maria and James *did* recruit him on the grounds that they obviously already *had* recruited him. Weird, but sometimes time-travel's a weird business, and if I were James and Maria, I'd never trust Baz out of my sight. It sounds risky to let him work for the Foundation, but one thing you can bet; he'll never get his hands on another TDD.

Lucky Old James

There were just a few things left to sort out. First, there were the time medallions. They were ruined, and James put them in the Foundation museum for safe keeping. Check.

Then, there was the sol-shot. Maria took that away from Baz and it went into the museum, too. Check.

Dr Pennyfather wanted to get into the museum, but James locked her out. It did me good to see Dr Pennyfather getting a taste of her own medicine. She also wanted to come on the next trip, but James wouldn't let her do that, either. She wanted to know everything about Kane and the Kane Foundation. For some reason she seemed really interested in Kane! James wouldn't tell her anything at all. Check and double-check.

I was beginning to like James, so I decided to leave him a present when we left. I had just the thing…

The last problem was what to do with Lizba's skull. James and Maria decided that it didn't belong in the museum. They couldn't let Dr Pennyfather keep it so, in the end, we went to the Asbestos Ranges, and then came back to the present. We climbed the hill and James very carefully dug up a small tree. He buried the skull in the hole and replanted the tree.

"Root in peace, Lizba," I said.

"Yes," said Coxie. "Rest in peace."

Then we all climbed down the hill again. On the way, we saw (and heard) a flock of sulphur-crested cockatoos, squawking and shrieking like a hundred Crackers. James looked up wistfully. "*Cacatua galerita*," he said. "Aren't they wonderful? What I wouldn't give for…"

"Don't even think about it," said Maria. "We're here to solve anomalies, not to create them."

Finally, we went back for Dr Pennyfather. She was *really* mad at being kept out of things. She wanted the skull back. She wanted exact details of my treatment, and on the workings of time-travel, and the development of the human race. She wanted to be taken back to the tenth century, and the first century, and to prehistoric times.

"Take her," advised Coxie. "Perhaps she'll be eaten by a dinosaur."

She *also* wanted to witness the beginning of human life, and to see the fiftieth century. She wanted to interview Kane. She wanted a hundred other things, too. I'm happy to report that she didn't get a single one of them. What she *did* get was a long lecture from James and the threat of having her memory vacuumed.

That shut her up.

We sorted out the final details of our story, and then we were ready to roll. At the last minute, I slipped quickly into the museum and left the present for James on the desk. Then, we left the Foundation and were zipped back to our own time.

There was a sort of blink, and then I was lying in the ambulance, with an ambulance attendant peering at me closely. "What's up?" I yelled, and sat up.

I tried to talk the attendants into letting me out of the ambulance, but no such luck. They carted me off to the hospital, then stuck me in the intensive-care unit. Mum and Dad came, and tried to find out what was going on, but nobody could explain. The ambulance attendant swore I'd stopped breathing, but every test proved that I was perfectly fit. All the same, they kept me in for another day, just to make sure. Coxie came to visit. We were eating our way through a big bunch of grapes when we heard a tapping sound at the door.

"Coxie, tell me it isn't who I think it is," I said.

"It is," said Coxie.

I laid down flat and folded my hands on my chest. "Tell her I've died."

Too late. Dr Pennyfather was already by the bed. "Hello, boys."

We stared at her, because there was something wrong with her voice. And something wrong with her face. She was trying to smile, I think.

"We have some matters to discuss, don't we, boys?" Out came three big notebooks, and I groaned. "First of all," she said, in a too sweet voice, "I must ask you to relate your own separate impressions of the future. Write down whatever you can remember. Don't discuss it beforehand, just write down whatever you recall. I shall do the same, and we'll compare the three accounts." She smiled again. "You are very privileged to be a part of this. Your help will be of immeasurable value to my paper."

Coxie and I glanced at one another, and I gave him a little nod.

"What paper, Dr Pennyfather?" he asked.

"My paper on temporal translation, and on the Kane Foundation," said Dr Pennyfather. "Physical evidence is lacking, but there *are* your test results, Tom. You are now fully recovered from your nerve-burn."

"My what?" I said.

"Your nerve-burn," repeated Dr Pennyfather.

Coxie and I shrugged. "I don't know anything about that, Dr Pennyfather," I said. "But thanks for coming in. And thanks for calling the ambulance. Apparently, I nearly choked on something. Good thing you were there, right?"

Dr Pennyfather's smile slipped. "I don't know what you two are up to, but I insist that you write those accounts now. I want every detail from the past weeks. Every detail you remember from the thirty-fifth century."

I laughed. "This is the twentieth century, not the thirty-fifth. What are you talking about?"

Dr Pennyfather practically ground her teeth. "I want to know everything about Dr Smith and his mother, about

121

that insufferable James and Maria and the Kane Foundation, about time-travel and its relationship to the opalized skull, and about nerve-burn and its causes and treatment. You must co-operate."

Coxie and I looked at her blankly. "What *is* she talking about?" I said to Coxie.

Dr Pennyfather was really angry, but there was really nothing she could do. She did try to get Sergeant Kerry to question me again about the theft of the skull, but after she started babbling on about time-travel, medallions, and ray guns, they dropped the whole case. Later, we heard the university had sacked her, on the grounds that her theories were unsound. I bet they'd been waiting for an excuse to do that for ages! These days, I hear she's working on the preservation of flora and fauna, and writing science fiction. She's also got married to some poor man. Oddly enough, his surname is Kane...

All this happened some time ago. For months, I used to jump every time a light flickered or a stranger looked at me, but now I've decided that it really is all over. By the end of the summer I'd grown a lot, and now I'm almost taller than Dad.

Sometimes I think about James and Maria and Baz. Sometimes I remember Lizba. I don't know exactly where her skull is buried, because the Asbestos Ranges are so vast and it was dark when we were there. But still, it's there in the hills where she died, with a healthy tree standing guard. And James and Maria are (will be) doing their best to keep time safe from people like Baz. I think that's what Lizba would have liked.

The other day, I was at Coxie's place. His sister, the Noise Machine, was pretending to be a jet, so Coxie and I were out at the parrot palace, with Cracker and his new friend Jojo, to get some peace. Cracker was swinging wildly on his perch, shrieking and showing off, and Jojo was cuddling up under Coxie's chin and chattering.

"Poor old James," said Coxie, out of the blue.

That was all he said, but I knew what he meant. "Hey, Coxie," I said. "What would you say if I told you one of Cracker's feathers had somehow found its way into the thirty-fifth century?"

A big smile spread over Coxie's face. "Feathers carry DNA, don't they?" he said.

"Yes. A whole sulphur-crested cockatoo blueprint in one little, white package. Hard to believe, isn't it?"

"Yes," said Coxie. "It's hard to believe." He put Jojo back on the perch, and Cracker jumped down to nibble on Coxie's ear.

"So, what would you say?" I asked.

"I'd say, lucky old James," said Coxie.

Time Line

3570 BC	Lizba Smith dies and the last set of time-travel medallions are destroyed.
3000 BC	Tom and Coxie meet Lizba and Tom is shot with a sol-shot.
AD 1700	Baz and Tom visit the site of Dr Pennyfather's future home.
AD 1990s	The active time-scheme. Tom and Coxie have the adventures related in *Timedetectors*. For adventures related in *A Theft in Time: Timedetectors II*, please see Magnified Time Line.
AD 3149	The sol-shot is invented.
AD 3151	The first case of nerve-burn is reported.
AD 3152	Lizba Smith is born.
AD 3155	Kane, founder of the Kane Foundation, is born.
AD 3160	Palmer, Lizba's partner in the creation of the time medallions, dies.
AD 3193	The original time medallions are destroyed.
AD 3195	Baz experiments with creating time-travel. The Kane Foundation is established.
AD 3201	Time-displacement devices (TDDs) are developed.
AD 3273	The germ-purge, in which the last specimens of *Cacatua galerita* are destroyed, is carried out.
AD 3430	James is born.
AD 3432	Maria is born.
AD 3453	Tom arrives in the future to be treated for nerve-burn.

Magnified Time Line

AD 1700   Baz and Tom visit the site of Dr
Pennyfather's future home.

AD 1990s   The active time-scheme.

May 3, 199_ Eighteen months before Day One.
James, Maria, Tom, and Coxie set a trap for Baz.

Day One   Tom telephones Sergeant Kerry in an attempt to find
the skull. Tom writes to Dr Pennyfather requesting a
meeting with her.

Day Nine   Baz and Tom enter Dr Pennyfather's house after
travelling to AD 1700 in order to break in.

Day Eleven   Tom arrives in Devonport.

9:00 a.m.	Tom arrives at Dr Pennyfather's house.
9:30 a.m.	Tom leaves Dr Pennyfather's house and is followed by Baz through the mall.
9:45 a.m.	Tom arrives at Coxie's house.
12:00 noon	Tom and Coxie meet Baz at the mall.
3:00 p.m.	Tom, Coxie, and Baz visit Dr Pennyfather's house.
5:00 p.m.	Tom and Coxie return to Coxie's. Tom is questioned by Sergeant Kerry.
7:00 p.m.	Tom and Coxie go to a movie.
7:45 p.m.	Dr Pennyfather questions Tom in the foyer of the movie theatre.
9:00 p.m.	Tom and Coxie leave the movie theatre and are chased by James and Maria. Baz appears and kidnaps Tom.
9:45 p.m.	Tom is left by Baz and collapses. Tom is taken into the future to be treated for nerve-burn.
11:30 p.m.	Tom is taken to hospital and his parents visit.

Day Twelve   Dr Pennyfather and Coxie visit Tom in hospital.

AD 3453   Tom arrives in the future to be treated for nerve-burn.

From the Authors

We live in Tasmania with our two children, and our family loves a good science-fiction story. At the end of our first time-travel adventure, *Timedetectors*, our heroes, Tom and Coxie, were left with a futuristic ray gun that no longer worked. What would happen, we wondered, if the weapon mysteriously recharged? Or if someone in the future decided the boys knew too much? We wrote *A Theft in Time: Timedetectors II* to find out.

Darrel and Sally Odgers

From the Illustrator

I grew up with one ambition – to be an artist. After I finished school, I started my first job, which was drawing boots and clothing for a surplus supply store. From there, I went on to drawing comic strips and illustrating and designing T-shirts and blankets. Finally, I began painting and illustrating children's books, which I have been doing for the past six years.

Richard Hoit

SOMETHING STRANGE
My Father the Mad Professor
A Theft in Time: Timedetectors II
CD and the Giant Cat
Chocolate!
White Elephants and Yellow Jackets
Dream Boat

WHEN THINGS GO WRONG
The Long Walk Home
The Trouble with Patrick
The Kids from Quiller's Bend
Laughter Is the Best Medicine
Wild Horses
The Sunday Horse

ANOTHER TIME, ANOTHER PLACE
Cloudcatcher
Flags
The Dinosaur Connection
Myth or Mystery?
Where Did the Maya Go?
The Journal: Dear Future II

CONFIDENCE AND COURAGE
Imagine This, James Robert
Follow That Spy!
Who Will Look Out for Danny?
Fuzz and the Glass Eye
Bald Eagles
Cottle Street

Written by **Darrel** and **Sally Odgers**
Illustrated by **Richard Hoit**
Edited by **David Nuss**
Designed by **Pat Madorin**

© 1997 Shortland Publications Limited
All rights reserved.

02 01 00 99 98 97
10 9 8 7 6 5 4 3 2 1

Published by Shortland Publications Limited, 2B Cawley Street,
Ellerslie, Auckland, New Zealand
Distributed in Australia by Rigby Heinemann, a division of
Reed International Books Australia Pty Ltd. ACN 001 002 357,
22 Salmon Street, Port Melbourne, Victoria 3207
Distributed in the United Kingdom by Kingscourt Publishing Limited,
P.O. Box 1427, Freepost, London W6 9BR

Printed by Colorcraft, Hong Kong
ISBN: 1-57257-679-0